ANTICHRISTA

AMÉLIE NOTHOMB

Antichrista

*Translated from the French
by Shaun Whiteside*

faber and faber

First published under the title *Antéchrista*
© Editions Albin Michel S.A. – Paris, 2003

First published in the UK in 2005
by Faber and Faber Limited
3 Queen Square London WC1N 3AU

Typeset in Bembo by Faber and Faber Limited
Printed in England by Mackays of Chatham, plc

A CIP record for this book
is available from the British Library

ISBN 0–571–22483–0

2 4 6 8 10 9 7 5 3 1

ANTICHRISTA

THAT FIRST DAY, I SAW HER SMILE. Immediately I wanted to know her.

I knew very well that I wouldn't. I wasn't capable of approaching her. I always waited for other people to approach me; no one ever came.

That was what university was: thinking you were going to open yourself up to a universe, and meeting nobody.

A week later, her eyes settled on me.

I thought they would turn away in a flash. But no: they stayed and weighed me up. I didn't dare return that gaze: the ground fell away beneath my feet, and I was short of breath.

It didn't stop, and the pain became unbearable. With unprecedented courage, I plunged my eyes into hers. She gave me a little wave and laughed.

Then I saw her talking to some boys.

The next day, she came over to me and said hello.

I said hello back, and nothing more. I hated my awkwardness.

'You look younger than the others,' she observed.

'That's because I am. I turned sixteen a month ago.'

'Me too. I turned sixteen three months ago. Admit it, you wouldn't have believed it.'

'You're right.'

Her confidence made up for the two or three years that separated us from the pack.

'What's your name?' she asked.

'Blanche. What about you?'

'Christa.'

Such an unusual name. Lost in wonder, I fell silent once again. She saw my astonishment and added:

'It's not so rare in Germany.'

'Are you German?'

'No. I come from the eastern cantons.'

'Do you speak German?'

'Of course.'

I looked at her admiringly.

'Bye, Blanche.'

I didn't have time to say goodbye to her. She had already gone down the steps of the lecture hall staircase. A gang of students hailed her noisily. Beaming, Christa walked towards the group that was calling to her.

'She's integrated,' I thought to myself.

It was a word of immense significance to me. I had never been integrated into anything at all. I felt a mixture of jealousy and contempt for those who were.

I had always been alone and wouldn't have minded had it been a matter of choice. It never had been. I dreamed of being integrated, if only to give myself the luxury of subsequently disintegrating.

More than anything else I dreamed of becoming Christa's friend. The idea of having a friend struck me as incredible, let alone being Christa's friend – but no, there was no point in hoping.

For a moment I wondered why that friendship seemed so desirable. I had no clear answer: there was something about that girl, but I couldn't tell what it was.

As I was leaving the grounds of the university, a voice called out my name.

That had never happened to me before, and it plunged me into a kind of panic. I turned around and saw Christa running to catch up with me. It was wonderful.

'Where are you going?' she asked, walking with me.

'Home.'

'Where do you live?'

'Five minutes' walk away.'

'I could do with that!'

'Why? Where do you live?'

'I told you: in the eastern cantons.'

'Don't tell me you go back there every evening.'

'I do.'

'But it's such a long way!'

'Yes: two hours by train to get here, two hours by train to get back. Not counting bus journeys. It's the only solution I've found.'

'Are you going to be able to keep it up?'

'We'll see.'

I didn't dare ask her any more questions for fear of putting her ill at ease. She probably couldn't afford student lodgings.

Outside my block, I said goodbye.

'Do you live with your parents?' she asked.

'Yes. Do you live with your parents as well?'

'Yes.'

'That's normal at our age,' I added, although I wasn't sure why.

She burst out laughing, as though I had said something ridiculous. I was ashamed of myself.

I didn't know if I was her friend. By what very mysterious criteria do you tell if you're someone's friend? I'd never had one.

For example, she had thought I was risible: was that a mark of friendship or contempt? It had hurt me, but only because I was already fond of her.

Taking advantage of a moment's lucidity, I wondered why. Was the little, the very little that I knew of her sufficient cause for my desire to please her? Or was it for the pathetic reason that she, alone of all her kind, had looked at me?

On Tuesday, lectures began at eight o'clock in the morning. Christa had huge rings under her eyes.

'You look tired,' I observed.

'I got up at four o'clock this morning.'

'Four o'clock! You told me the journey took two hours.'

4

'I don't live in Malmédy itself. My village is half an hour from the station. If I'm going to catch the five o'clock train it means getting up at four o'clock. And the university isn't exactly next door to the station in Brussels either.'

'Getting up at four o'clock in the morning isn't human.'

'Have you got a better answer?' she said irritably.

She turned on her heels.

I was furious with myself. I had to help her.

In the evening I talked to my parents about Christa. To serve my ends, I said she was my friend.

'You've got a friend?' my mother asked me, trying not to seem too surprised by the news.

'Yes. Could she spend Monday nights here? She lives in a village in the eastern cantons, and on Tuesdays she has to get up at four o'clock in the morning to get to lectures at eight o'clock.'

'Of course she can. We'll put the folding bed in your room.'

The next day, summoning up as much courage as I could, I mentioned the idea to Christa:

'If you want, you could stay with me on Monday nights.'

She looked at me, stunned and radiant. It was the loveliest moment of my life.

'Do you mean it?'

I immediately spoiled the situation by adding, 'My parents have agreed.'

She snorted. I'd said something ridiculous again.

'Will you come?'

The advantage was already reversed. I was no longer being useful to her: I was begging her.

'Yes, I'll come,' she replied, as though hinting that she was only doing it to please me.

That didn't stop me from being delighted and fervently waiting for Monday.

An only child, bad at friendship, I had never had anybody over to my house, let alone to sleep in my room. The prospect filled me with terrifying joy.

Monday came. Christa didn't show me any particular consideration. But I was enraptured to notice that she was carrying a rucksack: her things.

That day, lectures stopped at four o'clock in the afternoon. I waited for Christa at the bottom of the lecture hall. She took an incredibly long time to say goodbye to all her acquaintances. Then, at a leisurely pace, she joined me.

Not until we were out of the field of vision of the other students did she deign to speak to me — with a forced friendliness, as though to stress that she was doing me a favour.

When I opened the door of my deserted flat, my heart was beating so hard that I felt sick. Christa came in and looked around her. She whistled:

'Not bad!'

I felt absurdly proud.

'Where are your parents?' she asked me.

'At work.'

'What do they do?'

'They teach at a middle school. My father teaches Latin and Greek, my mother Biology.'

'I see.'

I would have liked to ask her what exactly it was that she saw. I didn't dare.

The flat wasn't luxurious, but it had a lot of charm.

'Show me your room!'

Very moved, I took her to my lair. It was unimpressive. She looked disappointed.

'It doesn't look like much,' she said.

'It's nice here, you'll see,' I commented slightly sadly.

She threw herself on my bed, leaving me with the folding one. I had certainly resolved to let her have mine; however, I'd have been happier if she hadn't launched a pre-emptive strike. I immediately reproached myself for having such base thoughts.

'Have you always slept here?'

'Yes. I've never lived anywhere else.'

'Have you got any brothers and sisters?'

'No. What about you?'

'I've got two brothers and two sisters. I'm the youngest. Show me your clothes.'

'Pardon?'

'Open your wardrobe!'

Stunned, I did so. Christa leapt to her feet to come and look.

Concluding her examination, she said: 'You haven't got one nice thing.'

She grabbed my only elegant item of clothing, a figure-hugging Chinese dress. Before my astounded eyes, she threw off her T-shirt, her jeans and her shoes.

'It's a tight dress,' she said, looking at it. 'I'd better take off my panties as well.'

And she stood in front of me as naked as the day she was born. She slipped on the dress and looked at herself in the big mirror. It suited her. She admired herself.

'I wonder what it looks like on you.'

The very thing I was dreading happened. She took off the dress and threw it to me.

'Put it on!'

I was frozen, dumbfounded.

'Put it on, I tell you!'

I couldn't utter a sound.

Christa's beaming eyes opened wide, as though she finally understood:

'Are you bothered that I'm naked?'

I shook my head.

'Then why don't you get undressed?'

I shook my head again.

'Of course you can! You have to!'

I had to?

'Come on, you're being stupid! Take your clothes off!'

'No.'

That 'no' was a victory for me.

'I did!'

'That doesn't mean I have to imitate you.'

'*That doesn't mean I have to imitate you!*' she mocked in a

8

grotesque voice.

Did I really speak like that?

'Come on, Blanche, we're all girls together!'

Silence.

'After all, I'm completely naked! And it's not doing me any harm!'

'That's your problem.'

'You're the one with a problem. You're not much fun, are you?'

She threw herself on me, laughing. I rolled myself up in a ball on the folding bed. She took off my shoes, unbuttoned my jeans with startling skill, tugged on them and managed to take off my panties at the same time. Fortunately I was wearing a long T-shirt that came halfway down my thigh.

I yelled.

She stopped and looked at me in astonishment.

'What's wrong with you? Are you mad?'

I was shivering convulsively.

'Stop touching me!'

'Okay. Then get undressed.'

'I can't.'

'If you don't do it, I will!' she threatened.

'Why are you torturing me?'

'You're ridiculous. It isn't torture! We're just girls!'

'Why do you need me to get undressed?'

She gave a curious reply:

'So that we're equal.'

As though I could be her equal! Sadly, I couldn't think of a retort.

'So you see, you've got to do it!' she said triumphantly.

Defeated, I saw that there was no way out. My hands caught the bottom of my T-shirt. Try as I might, I couldn't lift it up.

'I can't do it.'

'I've got plenty of time,' she said, without taking her scornful eyes off me.

I was sixteen years old. I owned nothing, neither material goods nor spiritual comfort. I had no friends, no love, I hadn't experienced anything. I had no ideas, I wasn't sure I had a soul. My body was all I possessed.

At the age of six, getting undressed is nothing. By the age of twenty-six, getting undressed is already an old habit.

At the age of sixteen, getting undressed is an act of deranged violence.

Why are you asking me to do that, Christa? Do you know what it means for me? Would you demand such a thing if you knew? Is it precisely because you do know that you're doing it?

I don't understand why I'm obeying you.

Sixteen years of solitude, of self-hatred, of unformulated fears, of ungratified desires, of pointless pain, of abortive anger and unexploited energy were all contained in my body.

Bodies have three possible kinds of beauty: strength, grace and plenitude. Some miraculous bodies manage to unite all three. On the contrary, mine didn't contain an ounce of any of those three wonders. Lack was its mother tongue: it expressed the absence of strength, the absence of grace and the absence of fullness. It was like a scream of hunger.

At least this body, which had never been exposed to the sun, agreed nicely with my first name: that scrawny thing was white, white as a porcelain blade with its edge turned inwards.

'Today or tomorrow?' said Christa, sitting on my bed and apparently enjoying herself enormously, enjoying every last crumb of my pain.

Then, to get it over with, and with the swift gesture of someone pulling the pin from a grenade, I peeled off my T-shirt and threw it on the floor, like Vercingetorix throwing his shield at Caesar's feet.

Everything within me screamed with horror. I had lost the little I had, the poor secret that was my body. It was literally a sacrifice. And it was terrible to see that my sacrifice was for nothing.

For Christa barely nodded. She studied me from top to toe. A single detail held her attention:

'But you have breasts!'

I thought I was dying. Hiding tears of rage that would only have intensified my absurdity, I said:

'Of course. What did you expect?'

'Consider yourself lucky. With your clothes on you're as flat as a fillet of plaice.'

Charmed by her comments, I leaned down to pick up the T-shirt.

'No! I want to see you in the Chinese dress.'

11

She held it out to me. I put it on.

'It looks better on me than you,' she concluded.

All of a sudden that dress seemed like an additional degree of nakedness. I hastily took it off.

Christa leapt up and went and stood next to me in front of the big mirror.

'Look! We're not the same shape!' she exclaimed.

'Don't go on,' I said.

I was being tortured.

'Don't look away,' she ordered. 'Look at us.'

The comparison was overwhelming.

'You should develop your breasts,' she said in a learned voice.

'I'm only sixteen,' I protested.

'Yeah? So am I! And mine are a bit different, aren't they?'

'Each to his own.'

'No question! I'm going to teach you an exercise. My sister was like you. After six months of these exercises, she had changed, believe me. Okay, do as I do: one, two, one, two . . .'

'Clear off, Christa,' I said, going to get my T-shirt.

She pounced on it and took it to the other end of the room. I started after her. She was yelling with laughter. I was so furious and humiliated that it didn't occur to me to get another T-shirt from my wardrobe. Christa ran across the room, teasing me with her beautiful, triumphant body.

Just then my mother came back from work. She heard shrill cries coming from my room. She dashed over, opened the door without knocking and had the vision of two naked adolescent girls galloping in all directions. She didn't notice that one of them, her daughter, was close to tears. She had eyes only for the laughing stranger.

The moment my mother entered the place of my sacrifice, Christa's demonic laughter became the embodiment of freshness — hearty laughter, as healthy as her body. She stopped running and walked over to my mother, holding out her hand.

'Hi. Forgive me, I wanted to see what shape your daughter was.'

And she laughed, mischievous and delicious. My mother, thunderstruck, looked at this naked adolescent girl who was shaking her hand without the slightest embarrassment. After a moment's hesitation, she seemed to think the stranger was a child, and that she was very funny.

'So you're Christa?' she said, starting to laugh.

And they laughed and they laughed, as though the scene was the funniest thing in the world.

I watched my mother laugh, with a sense of having lost an ally.

I knew that the scene had been horrible rather than comical. I knew that Christa was only a child, that it was her strategy to win my mother over.

And I saw that my mother, without thinking anything amiss, saw the girl's beautiful body, full of life — and I knew that she was already wondering why mine wasn't as good.

My mother left. As soon as the door had shut behind her, Christa's laughter faded away.

'I've done you a favour,' she said. 'From now on you'll have no problems with nakedness.'

I thought that, in the general interest, I would try to believe that version of the terrible moment. I already knew I wouldn't be able to do it: when we were naked, side by side, facing the mirror, I had been too keenly aware of Christa's delight – her delight at humiliating me, her delight at her domination and her particular delight at seeing how much pain I suffered from being undressed, a distress that she absorbed through the pores of her skin and from which she drew a vivisectionist's delight.

'Your mother's beautiful,' she announced, putting her clothes back on.

'Yes,' I replied, surprised to hear her saying something nice.

'How old is she?'

'Forty-five.'

'She looks much younger.'

'That's true,' I observed proudly.

'What's her name?'

'Michelle.'

'And your father?'

'François.'

'What's he like?'

'You'll see. He'll be here this evening. What are your parents like?'

'Very different from yours.'

'What do they do?'

'How nosy you are!'

'But . . . you asked me the same thing about mine!'

'No. You were the one who felt the need to tell me your parents were teachers.'

I fell silent, astonished that she could be so disingenuous. And if I understood her correctly, she thought I was proud of the job my parents did. Ludicrous idea!

'You shouldn't dress like that,' she said again. 'You can't see your figure.'

'I don't follow. First of all you go off into ecstasies about the fact that I've got breasts, then you're indignant because they're not big enough, and now you're telling me to show them to you. You've lost me now.'

'You're so sensitive!'

And she smiled sarcastically.

Under normal circumstances my parents and I ate by ourselves, one at the kitchen table, another in front of the television, another sitting on her bed with a tray.

That evening, as we had a guest, my mother thought it might be a good idea to make a real dinner and sit down at the table together. When she called us, I sighed with relief at the idea of no longer being alone with my executioner.

'Good evening, *mademoiselle*,' said my father.

'Call me Christa,' she replied with extraordinary ease and a luminous smile.

She went over to him and, to his surprise and mine, plonked two great kisses on his cheeks. I could see that my father was charmed and surprised.

15

'It's nice of you to put me up for the night. You've got a fantastic flat.'

'Let's not exaggerate. We've just done it up nicely. If you'd seen the state we found it in, twenty years ago! My wife and I . . .'

And he set off on an interminable story in the course of which he spared us not a single detail of the fastidious work that had been done. Christa hung on his every word, as though his story was the most exciting thing she had ever heard.

'It's delicious,' she said as she took the plate that my mother held out to her.

My parents were delighted.

'Blanche told us you lived over by Malmédy.'

'Yes, I spend four hours a day on the train, not to mention the bus journeys.'

'Couldn't you rent a room on campus?'

'That's my goal. I'm working hard to get there.'

'You work?'

'Yes, I'm a waitress in a bar in Malmédy at the weekend, and sometimes during the week as well, when I don't get home too late. I'm paying for my studies myself.'

My parents gazed at her admiringly and, a minute later, looked with disapproval at their daughter who, at the age of sixteen, couldn't be bothered to attain financial independence.

'What do your parents do?' my father asked.

I exulted at the idea that she might reply, as she had to me: 'How nosy you are!'

16

Sadly, Christa, after a very studied little silence, announced with tragic simplicity:

'I come from a disadvantaged background.'

And she lowered her eyes.

I saw that she'd just gone up ten points in the polls.

Immediately afterwards, with the spirit of a bravely modest girl, she announced:

'If I've got my sums right, by the end of spring I should be able to rent a place.'

'But that's exactly when you'll be revising for your exams! You won't be able to get enough work done!' said my mother.

'There's no way around it,' she replied.

I wanted to slap her. I put it down to my evil nature and was furious with myself.

Cheerfully, Christa started talking again:

'You know what I'd really like? I'd like us to talk to each other informally – as long as you'll let me. It's true, you're young; I feel stupid addressing you politely.'

'If you like,' my father said, using the familiar *tu* and grinning from ear to ear.

I found her unbelievably brazen and was furious that my parents had allowed themselves to be seduced by her.

As she reached our room, she kissed my mother, saying:

'Good night, Michelle.'

And then my father:

'Good night, François.'

I regretted having given her their first names, as a torture victim regrets giving the names of his cell.

'Your father's not bad either,' she announced.

I realized that her compliments no longer delighted me.

She lay down on my bed and said, 'I'm happy to be here, you know.'

She laid her head on the pillow and was out like a light.

Her last words touched me and left me deeply perplexed. Had I misjudged Christa? Was my resentment about her well-founded?

My mother had seen us both naked, and she hadn't been shocked. Maybe she'd noticed that I had a problem with my body; maybe she'd thought that such behaviour would do me good.

Christa seemed to have some sort of complex about her origins. I shouldn't be angry with her for giving me a strange answer to my question. Her irrational attitude was merely an expression of her discomfort.

Finally, it was true that she deserved admiration for pursuing her studies all on her own, and at such a tender age. Rather than being meanly irritated about it, I would have to esteem her more highly and see her as a role model. I had been mistaken all along. I was ashamed not to have worked out straight away that Christa was a fantastic girl and that having her as a friend was an unexpected joy.

Those thoughts calmed me down.

The following morning, she thanked my parents effusively:

'Thanks to you, I was able to get three and a half hours more sleep than usual!'

On the way to university, she didn't say a word to me. I

thought she must have got out of the wrong side of bed.

The moment we arrived in the lecture hall I ceased to exist for her. I spent the day alone, as usual. Christa's laugh sometimes rang out in the distance. I was no longer quite sure that she had even slept in my room.

That evening, my mother declared:

'Your Christa is a find! She's incredible, funny, witty, full of life . . .'

My father butted in:

'And so mature! So brave! So intelligent! Such a judge of character!'

'Isn't she?' I said, scouring my memories for anything especially penetrating that Christa might have come out with.

'It took you a long time to find a friend, but given the quality of the one you've brought us, I finally understand: you had set the bar very high,' my mother went on.

'And she's beautiful,' exclaimed my progenitor.

'My goodness, that's so true,' observed his wife. 'And you haven't seen her naked.'

'Really? What's she like?'

'A very pretty piece, if you want my opinion.'

Dying of embarrassment, I broke in:

'Mum, please . . .'

'You're so uptight! Your friend showed herself to me without a care in the world, and she was right to do so. If she could cure you of your pathological prudery, it would be perfect.'

'Yes. And she could set you an example in other areas as well.'

It took me a considerable effort to contain my fury. I merely said:

'I'm happy that you liked Christa.'

'We love her! She can come here whenever she likes! Tell her that.'

'You can count on me.'

Back in my room, I undressed in front of the big mirror and looked myself up and down. My body insulted me. I couldn't help feeling that Christa hadn't been quite mean enough.

Since puberty, I had hated my body. I realized that Christa's gaze had made the situation worse; I could only see myself through her eyes and I hated myself.

Breasts are the biggest obsession of teenage girls: they've had them for so short a time that they can't quite get over them. The change in the hips is less of a surprise. It's a change rather than an addition. Those protuberances sprouting on girls' chests are strangers for a long time.

To make matters worse, that was the only part of my body that Christa had mentioned: further proof, if proof was needed, that it was my main problem. I tried out an experiment; I concealed my breasts in my hands and looked at myself: suddenly, I was acceptable and even quite pretty. I stopped hiding my chest, and immediately my appearance became pitiful, wretched, as though that failure contaminated everything else.

20

A voice in my head came to my defence:

'Well? You haven't finished growing. There are advantages to having small ones, too. Before Christa looked at you, you couldn't have cared less. Why do you set such store by that girl's judgement?'

In the mirror, I saw my shoulders and my arms adopting the position Christa suggested and performing the exercises that she had recommended for me.

The voice in my head yelled:

'No! Don't obey! Stop!'

My body submissively continued with its gymnastics.

I promised myself never to start doing them again.

The next day I resolved to stop approaching Christa. She must have been aware of it, because it was she who approached me; she kissed me and looked at me in silence. I was so ill at ease that I started talking:

'My parents want me to tell you that they adore you and that you can come back to ours whenever you want.'

'I adore your parents, too. Tell them I'm pleased.'

'And will you come back?'

'Next Monday.'

Some loud voices called out to her. She turned round and headed towards her gang. She sat down on one guy's knees; the others bellowed to her to do the same to them.

It was Wednesday. Next Monday was still a long way off. I no longer felt I was in so much of a hurry. Wasn't I better off without her than with her?

Sadly, I couldn't be sure of that. Being without her meant

being more alone than anyone. My loneliness had worsened since meeting Christa: when the girl wasn't aware of my existence, it wasn't loneliness that I suffered from, but dereliction. I was abandoned.

Or worse: I was being punished. If she didn't come and talk to me, wasn't it because I'd made a mistake? And I spent hours brooding over my behaviour. I was searching for something that deserved punishment whose justification had escaped me, while I remained convinced of its rightness.

The following Monday my parents welcomed Christa excitedly. They served champagne; she said she had never drunk it in her life.

It was a jovial evening: Christa babbled, interrogated my father or my mother on the most diverse subjects, exploded with laughter at their replies and slapped me on the thigh to call me to witness, increasing the general mirth, from which I felt increasingly excluded.

It seemed to me that the limit was reached when Christa, noticing my mother's elegance, began to sing the Beatles song, 'Michelle, ma belle . . .' I was about to explode that things couldn't get much more ridiculous, when I saw that my mother was delighted. It's terrible when you realize that your parents have lost their dignity.

It was when she talked to them that I found out about the life of the girl who was supposed to be my friend:

'Yes, I've got a boyfriend. His name's Detlev and he lives in Malmédy. He works in the same bar as me. He's eighteen. I'd like him to learn a trade.'

22

Or:

'All my mates from school went straight into the factory. I was the only one who continued my education. Why political science? Because I have an ideal of social justice. I'd like to know how to help my own kind.'

(That won her another ten points in the polls. Why did she always talk as though she was in the middle of an election campaign?)

At that moment, Christa cruelly sensed something. She turned to me and asked me:

'Basically, Blanche, you've never told me why you were studying political science.'

Had I had the presence of mind, I would have replied, 'I've never told you because you've never asked.' Unfortunately, I was too stunned to speak: I was so unused to her speaking to me.

Appalled at my dazed appearance, my father pressed me:

'Come on, tell us, Blanche.'

I started stammering:

'I think it's interesting to learn how to live with human beings . . .'

I had not expressed it well, but that was the underlying foundation of my thoughts, and it struck me as a valid point of view. My parents sighed. I understood that Christa had questioned me simply with a view to humiliating me in front of them. She had succeeded: in their eyes, I didn't come up to the ankles of this 'admirable girl'.

'Blanche has always been too good,' said my mother.

'You'll have to take her out for us,' my father continued.

23

I shivered; the full horror of our *ménage à quatre* lay in those three pronouns: 'you . . . her . . . us . . .' I had become the third person. When you talk about someone in the third person, it means they aren't there. Effectively, I wasn't there. Things were only happening between these people 'you' and 'us'.

'Yes, Christa. Teach her a bit about life,' added my mother.

'I'll try,' the girl replied.

I bit the dust.

A few days later at university Christa came looking for me, a bored expression on her face.

'I promised your parents I'd introduce you to my friends,' she said.

'It's kind of you, but I'm not keen on the idea.'

'Hurry up, I've got other things to do.'

She pulled me by the arm and threw me towards a cluster of big oafs:

'Guys, this is Blanche.'

To my great relief no one noticed me. That was it: I had been introduced.

Christa had done her duty. She turned her back on me and started talking to some other people. I stood alone among her gang; my discomfort was palpable.

I walked away, drenched in cold sweat. I was aware of the idiotic thing that had just happened: so tiny an incident that it had to be forgotten straight away. But I couldn't shake off the feeling of being in a nightmare.

The professor came into the lecture hall. The students

immediately took their seats. As she passed by me, Christa leaned over for long enough to murmur in my ear:

'You! I went to a hell of a lot of bother for you, and you just move off without speaking to anyone.'

She sat down two rows away, leaving me frozen and shattered.

I started losing sleep.

I became convinced that Christa was right; it was less painful. Yes, I should have tried to speak to someone. But to say what? I had nothing to say? And to whom? I didn't want to know those people.

— *You see? You don't know anything about them and already you've decided you don't want to know them. How contemptuous and haughty you are! Christa is generous: she approaches others, as she approached you, as she approached your parents. She has something to offer everyone. You haven't got anything for anyone, not even yourself. You are a void. Christa may be a little abrupt, but at least she exists. Anything would be better than being you.*

Discordant words creaked around my head: *Stop! How dare she say that she's gone to a hell of a lot of bother for you? Introductions go in both directions: she didn't tell you anyone's name. She doesn't give a damn about you.*

The inner reply thundered: *You are so up yourself! No one introduced her to anyone. She came on her own, from her remote little province, she's the same age as you and she doesn't need help from anyone. The truth is that you're behaving like an idiot.*

Protests from the adverse party: *So? Has anyone heard me complaining? I'm happy to be alone. I prefer my solitude to her*

25

promiscuity. It's my right.

Yells of laughter: *Liar! You know you're lying! You've always dreamed of being integrated, especially since it's never happened to you! Christa is the opportunity of a lifetime! And you're busy missing it, you wretch, you . . .*

Insults of the worst kind followed, all directed at me.

That was the rule with my insomnia: I hated myself to the point of no return.

On Monday night, in my room, I asked Christa:

'Tell me about Detlev.'

I was worried that she would come out with that phrase 'None of your business!', the one she was so good at.

But no; she looked at the ceiling and said in a far-off voice:

'Detlev . . . He smokes. In a really classy way. He's got charisma. Tall, fair. A bit like David Bowie. He has a past: he's suffered. When he walks into a room, the people fall silent and look at him. He doesn't talk much, he doesn't smile much. He's not the kind to let his feelings show.'

This portrait of a brooding, handsome man struck me as utterly ridiculous, apart from one detail that had captured my attention:

'Does he really look like David Bowie?'

'Especially when he's making love.'

'Have you ever seen David Bowie making love?'

'Don't be stupid, Blanche,' she sighed exasperatedly.

But my question seemed perfectly logical to me. Probably to avenge herself, she yelled:

26

'You're clearly a virgin.'

'How do you know?'

Stupid question. She burst out laughing. Once again I'd missed a terrific opportunity to keep my mouth shut.

'Does he love you?' I asked.

'Yes. Too much.'

'Why too much?'

'You don't know what it's like to have a guy gazing at you all the time as though you were a goddess.'

That 'you don't know what it's like' was supremely contemptuous. The rest of the sentence seemed simply grotesque: poor Christa, who had to endure the cruel fate of being devoured by the eyes of David Bowie! What a poser!

'All you need to do is tell him to love you less,' I suggested, taking her at her word.

'Did I ask your advice? He can't help it.'

I pretended to have a bright idea.

'You could show him the contents of your handkerchief. He wouldn't be quite so much in love after that.'

'You're sad, you really do have a problem,' she said dismissively.

And she turned out the light to indicate that she wanted to go to sleep.

My mental associate levelled accusations at me: *You can find her as daft as you like, it doesn't matter: you'd still like to be in her place. She's loved, she has experience, and you're a dope who risks never having any of that.*

And then there was the question of love. At the age of

sixteen, it was quite possible that I'd never known it. Sadly I wasn't even as greedy as that: if only I could have experienced a form of love of any kind at all! My parents had only ever had affection for me, and I was busy discovering how precarious that was. I had brought home a seductive girl, and now I was a dead weight in their hearts. It had taken nothing more than that.

I spent the night scouring my memory: had anyone ever loved me? Had I ever encountered anyone, child or adult, who had made me feel the incredible sense of election that comes with love? However much I might have wished, I had never experienced the grandiloquent friendships of ten-year-old girls; at secondary school I had never received a teacher's passionate attention. I had never seen anyone's eyes light up with that flame that consoles us for being alive.

So, it was easy for me to mock Christa. She might have been pretentious and vain and silly, but at least she attracted love. And I remembered the psalm: 'Blessed be those who inspire love.'

Yes, blessed be they, for even if they had all the shortcomings in the world, they were still the salt of the earth, the earth where I counted for nothing, where I hadn't even been noticed.

Why was that so? If I hadn't loved, it would have been perfectly fair. And yet the opposite was the case: I had always been perfectly willing to love. Since earliest childhood, I had stopped counting the number of little girls to whom I had offered my heart and who had turned it down flat; reaching adolescence, I had swooned over a boy who had never noticed I existed. And those had been excesses of love; plain affection had met with stubborn rejection.

Christa was right: I must have a problem. What was it? It wasn't that I was all that ugly. And anyway, I had seen ugly girls who received their share of love.

I remembered an episode from my teenage years which perhaps contained the elusive clue. I didn't have far to seek: it had happened the year before. I was fifteen and unhappy because I didn't have enough friendship in my life. In my final-year class there were three inseparable girls: Valérie, Chantal and Patricia. There was nothing extraordinary about them, apart from the fact that they were always together, and that seemed to make them very happy.

I dreamed of joining that group. I started going around with them wherever they went: for months, the trio were never seen without me in their midst. I kept joining in with their conversations. Of course, I noticed that they didn't reply when I asked them a question; but I was patient and settled for what I had, which struck me as a great deal: the right to be there.

Six months later, after an explosion of mirth, Chantal uttered this horrible sentence:

'We three make up an incredible gang!'

And all three collapsed with laughter.

And yet, as always, I was there among them. It was a dagger in my heart. I understood the abject truth: I didn't exist. I had never existed.

I was never seen with the trio again. The girls noticed my absence no more than they had my presence. I was invisible.

That was my problem.

Lack of visibility or lack of existence? It came down to the same thing: I wasn't there.

The memory tormented me. I realized with disgust that nothing had changed.

Or rather it had: there was Christa. Christa who had seen me. No, that would have been too wonderful. Christa hadn't seen me: she had seen my problem. And she was exploiting it.

She had seen a girl who was suffering most terribly from non-existence. She had understood that she could use that sixteen-year-old pain.

She had already taken over my parents and their flat. And, having come this far, she certainly wasn't about to stop.

The following Monday, Christa didn't come to lectures, so I came home on my own.

My mother immediately noticed that Christa wasn't there and asked me a hundred questions:

'Is she ill?'

'I have no idea.'

'What do you mean you have no idea?'

'Just that. She didn't tell me.'

'And didn't you phone her?'

'I haven't got her number.'

'Have you never asked her?'

'She doesn't like me to ask her questions about her family.'

'So you didn't get her number.'

My fault again.

'She could call,' I said. 'She's got ours.'

30

'It's probably too expensive for her parents.'

My mother was never lost for an excuse for the girl who was supposed to be my friend.

'You haven't even got her address? Or the name of her village? You're pretty clueless!'

My mother wasn't going to give up and decided to try directory enquiries.

'A family called Bildung, somewhere around Malmédy . . . Nothing? Fine. Thanks.'

My father came home, and his wife told him about her search and my lack of presence of mind.

'Honestly!' he said to me.

The evening was grim.

'You haven't had a row with her, have you?' my mother asked me in a cross voice.

'No.'

'For once in your life you've got a friend! A fantastic girl!' she went on accusingly.

'Mum, I told you, I haven't had a row.'

I worked out in passing that my parents would never forgive me any rift I might have had with her.

My father couldn't eat a mouthful of the lovely meal prepared for Christa.

'She might have had an accident,' he said finally. 'Or perhaps she's been kidnapped!'

'Do you think so?' my mother asked fearfully.

Exasperated, I retired to my bedroom. They didn't notice. The next day, Christa was chatting with her gang. I charged over:

'Where were you?'

'What are you talking about?'

'Last night. It was Monday, we were waiting for you.'

'Oh, yes. Detlev and I were out too late. I couldn't get up in the morning.'

'Why didn't you let me know?'

'Oh my, is it that serious?' she sighed.

'My parents were worried.'

'That's sweet of them. Will you apologize for me?'

And she turned her back on me, to show that she wasn't going to waste any more time in my company.

That evening I explained the situation as best I could to my parents. They were boundlessly indulgent of Christa and thought the situation entirely natural. They quickly asked me if she would be coming the following Monday.

'I think so,' I replied.

They were terribly pleased.

'You see,' my mother said to my father. 'She's safe and sound.'

And, in fact, the following Monday she did come home with me. My parents gave her an even warmer welcome.

'Her trick has worked,' I thought.

I had no idea how true that was. I saw it over dinner, when my father spoke:

'Christa, Michelle and I have been thinking. We'd like to suggest that you come and live here with us during the week. You would share Blanche's room. At the weekend you would go back to your own home in Malmédy.'

'François, don't try and take over Christa's life!' interrupted my mother.

'You're right, I'm jumping the gun. You're free to refuse, Christa. But all three of us would be absolutely delighted.'

I listened to him with an aching heart.

With consummate artistry, Christa lowered her eyes.

'I can't accept . . .' she murmured.

I held my breath.

'Why?' my father asked anxiously.

She pretended to overcome a long series of scruples before replying:

'I couldn't pay you any rent . . .'

'There's never been any question of that,' my mother protested.

'No, I just can't. It's too generous of you . . .'

That was my opinion too.

'You're joking!' said my father. 'The generosity would be all yours! We're so happy when you're here! Blanche is transformed! You're like a sister to her!'

It was so outrageous that I nearly burst out laughing.

Christa looked at me shyly.

'Blanche, you need your privacy in your own room. That's normal.'

I was about to reply when my mother cut in:

'You should have seen how upset Blanche was last week when you didn't come. She's never been good at making friends, you know. So it would be beyond her wildest dreams if you accepted.'

'Go on, Christa, it would make us all so happy,' my father insisted.

'In that case I can't refuse,' she agreed.

Before accepting, she had waited until we all had to thank her.

My mother came over and kissed Christa, who wrinkled her nose with pleasure. My father beamed.

I was an orphan.

I received confirmation of this a little later, in the kitchen, when I was helping my father to put the washing-up away. Knowing that Christa wouldn't be able to hear us, I asked him:

'Why didn't you ask my opinion?'

I imagined that he was going to give me the legitimate reply: 'It's my house, I can invite anyone I like.'

And yet this is what he said:

'She isn't just your friend. She's ours, too.'

I was on the point of correcting him, to say that she was *only* theirs, when Christa bounded in, giving frenzied emphasis to the portion of childhood that she was still able to claim.

'I'm so happy!' she cried.

And she threw herself into my father's arms, then kissed me on both cheeks.

'François, Blanche, you're my family now!'

My mother came and joined us lest she miss any of this charming tableau. The girl of their dreams laughed with joy, hopped up and down and threw her arms around my parents, who were touched by her virginal freshness. The scene struck me as utterly ridiculous, and I was dismayed by my isolation. I spoke a bit frostily:

'And what about Detlev?'

'I'll see him at weekends.'

'Will that be enough for you?'

'Of course.'

'And will it suit him?'

'You're not suggesting that I should ask his permission?'

'Good for you, Christa!' my mother rejoiced.

'How old-fashioned you are!' my father said to me.

They hadn't understood a thing. I wasn't talking about freedom or permission. I had this notion of passionate love: if it ever happened to me, I wouldn't be able to imagine a moment's separation. What could you bear to have between the loved one and yourself, apart from the blade of a sword? I was careful not to voice opinions that I guessed would bring torrents of mockery down on my head.

And I gravely watched Christa's new parents celebrating the catastrophe.

On Tuesday, the schemer had to return to her province to fetch some of her belongings.

That night I savoured the solitude of my room with tragic delight. You didn't really own the little you thought you did, or rather your possession of it was so precarious that its expropriation was lethal. That treasure-house of neglected girls, the dream space of a room of one's own, even that was going to be taken from me.

I didn't sleep. I was filled with the idea of what I was about to lose. My sanctuary since I was born, the temple of my childhood, the resonance chamber of my adolescent howls.

Christa had said that my room 'didn't look like much'. And she was quite right: that was because it looked like me. Its walls did not bear portraits of singers or posters of evanescent, diaphanous creatures: they were as bare as the interior of my being. But neither was there anything to suggest that I was ahead of my years: I wasn't. There were piles of books here and there: they took the place of an identity.

The insignificance that was so precious to me was about to be invaded in the name of a friendship that didn't actually exist, and which I would nonetheless have to feign rather than lose the last vestiges of my parents' affection.

My hectoring internal dialogue resumed: *How small your universe is, how tiny your problems; think of those who haven't got a bedroom, and besides, she'll teach you about life, Christa, it isn't going to be a luxury.*

These well-meant observations didn't convince me in the slightest.

On Wednesday afternoon, the invader descended upon us with a huge bag that didn't bode well – and that was only the start: from it she took endless clothes, a ghetto-blaster and CDs whose titles frightened the life out of me, some knick-knacks that were clearly supposed to be endearing and, horror of horrors, some rolled-up posters.

'You're finally going to have a young person's room!' Christa exclaimed.

And over the walls she spread the faces of individuals whose fame I had until that point been spared and to which I would henceforth be exposed. I promised myself to forget their names.

The room echoed with hideous lamentations and blandly well-intentioned lyrics, and she was even tasteless enough to sing along.

She had got off to a flying start.

Christa couldn't bear to listen to an album all the way through to the end: she was forever changing them. There was a form of torture in the process: in fact, when she interrupted a disc, preferably in the middle of a track, my hope returned. I told myself that she might finally have noticed how wretchedly awful that song had been; alas, upon hearing her new 'musical' selection, I immediately longed for the one I had just heard, at the same time forcing myself to try to appreciate this one, bearing in mind what the next one would probably be like.

'Isn't that great?' she would ask after half an hour of unbearable torment.

It seemed like an inane question to me. Since when were torturers concerned about their victims' opinions?

Was I capable of lying? Yes, I was.

'Fantastic. Especially German rock,' I was shocked to hear myself saying.

German rock was without a doubt the worst thing that Christa had inflicted on me. Did that mean I was such a masochist that I could declare a liking for something that in truth I found utterly repellent? On second thoughts, no. First of all, if you were going to listen to horrendous things, you might as well pursue the horror to its conclusion: touching bottom is less frightening than staying on the surface of abjection. And hideous as German rock might have been, it was incontestably superior to the French songsters in at least one respect: I couldn't make out the words.

'You're right, it's brilliant! Detlev and I absolutely love it,' she cried excitedly.

And she put on, at full blast, a piece delicately entitled 'So Schrecklich'. Couldn't have put it better myself, I thought. If any culture had produced composers of genius, then German culture had. So what had happened to make contemporary Teutonic musical creation the ugliest in the world? And as to Detlev and Christa's love life, accompanied by these inept and obnoxious anthems, it was clearly very far removed from Lohengrin and his swan.

Someone knocked timidly at the door. It was my father.

'Evening, François!' yelled Christa, smiling from ear to ear. 'All right?'

The idea of her being so familiar to my parents and calling them by their first names still struck me as weird.

'Yes, fine. Do forgive me, but isn't the music a little bit loud?' he stammered.

'You're right,' she said, turning it down. 'It was just to please Blanche: it's her favourite kind of music.'

'Ah,' he said, looking at me in puzzlement.

And off he went.

So not only did she have to subject me to that auditory punishment, she also had to convince everyone around me that I was the one chiefly responsible for this aural outrage.

At university, she brought me more actively into her gang. It had become essential.

'I'm living with Blanche now. She's sixteen, like me.'

'So you're sixteen, Christa?' a student asked.

'Well, yes.'

'You don't look it.'

'Blanche looks it, doesn't she?'

'Yeah,' said the guy, who couldn't have cared less one way or the other. 'How come you got into university at sixteen, Christa?'

'You see, where I come from, life is hard. I felt the need to grow up more quickly so that I could leave, free myself, grow my own wings, you understand?'

One of the things that annoyed me about her was that way she had of coming out with perfectly obvious phrases and finishing them with 'you understand?', as though the person she was speaking to had not grasped the subtlety of her discourse.

'I understand,' her friend replied.

'You're an amazing woman,' announced a tall, hairy guy.

'Blanche is different,' Christa continued. 'Her father and mother are teachers, so obviously she's studious. And she had never had a friend before me. She was so bored that she ended up top of the class.'

The boys in her gang gave a little snort of contempt.

I preferred not to show that I was offended. What could she claim to know of my life? And what gave her the right to serve me up as fodder for her mates' mockery? What need in her did it satisfy?

I had already worked out that Christa devoted the bulk of her time to self-promotion. And doubtless she found it more efficient to have a foil for the purpose: me.

And she really had struck lucky: thanks to me, she was housed, fed and laundered, at no cost other than my public ridicule, which also served her interests.

So she was plugging away at her image as a brave, deserving girl, advanced for her years, smart, etc., to the detriment of a silly, dozy clod from a 'privileged' background – by some sleight of hand she had managed to suggest that having teacher parents was a sign of incredible affluence.

The evening after that charming scene with her friends, she declared:

'Thanks to me, you're integrated now.'

No doubt she expected me to thank her. I didn't say a word.

Until I met Christa, one of the joys of my teenage life had consisted in reading: I lay down on my bed with a book and I became the text. If the novel was a good one, I became it. If it was mediocre, I still spent marvellous hours enjoying what I didn't like about it, smiling at missed opportunities.

Reading isn't a displacement activity, a substitute

40

pleasure. Seen from outside, my life was a skeleton; seen from within, it was like a house furnished only with an enormous library: the kind of interior that would provoke a mixture of envy and admiration for its lack of superfluity, its abundance of necessity.

No one knew me from within; no one knew that there was no need to feel sorry for me, no one apart from myself – and that was enough for me. I took advantage of my invisibility to spend whole days reading, unnoticed by anyone.

Except by my parents. I endured their sarcastic remarks: my biologist mother was offended that I was letting my body go to waste; my father backed her up with Latin and Greek quotations – *mens sana in corpore sano*, etc. – talked to me about Sparta and doubtless imagined that there were gymnasia where I could have gone to train in discus throwing. He would rather have fathered an Alcibiades than this dreamy, solitary girl, lost in literature.

I didn't try to defend myself. What was the point in trying to explain that I was invisible? They thought I was haughty and disdainful of the ordinary pleasures of my age group: I would have loved to find a set of directions for my teenage years, but without someone looking at me, that was out of the question. My parents didn't look at me, because they had already decreed what I was like 'too well-behaved, not lively enough, etc.'. Real looking has no preconceptions. If real eyes had rested on me, they would have seen an atomic battery, a bow stretched to its limits, awaiting nothing but an arrow and a target and wailing its desire for those twin treasures.

But while those favours were withheld, I didn't feel frustrated about the fact that I was blossoming in books: I was biding my time, weaving my petals around Stendhal and Radiguet, hardly the worst ingredients in the world. I wasn't selling myself short.

Since Christa had come, reading was like coitus interruptus: if she caught me reading, she told me off ('always with your nose in a book!'), then started talking to me about a thousand things which were of no interest whatsoever and which she invariably repeated four times. Since I grew bored to death as she jabbered on, I had no diversion but to count her repetitions and register my surprise at that fourfold cycle.

'And Marie-Rose said to me . . . then I said to Marie-Rose . . . It's unbelievable what Marie-Rose said, isn't it . . . Well, as you can imagine, I said to Marie-Rose, I said . . .'

Sometimes I forced myself, out of politeness, to feign a reaction, such as:

'Who's Marie-Rose?'

Bad idea. Christa was exasperated.

'I've told you a thousand times already!'

In actual fact she had probably mentioned this person *four* thousand times, to my recurrent boredom, and I must have forgotten every single one.

In short, it was better for me to keep my mouth shut and watch her talk, punctuating her speech with 'mmms' or nods of the head. But I found myself wondering why it was that she behaved like that: she wasn't an idiot, she couldn't possibly have found it amusing to come out with all this bilge that stood in for a story. I had come to the conclusion that Christa suffered from pathological jealousy: when she saw me being happy with a book, she had to destroy that happiness, since she was unable to appropriate it. She had managed to take over both my parents and the flat, so she needed my joys as well. And yet I was ready to share them with her.

'If you let me finish reading, I'll lend you this book.'

She couldn't wait and grabbed it out of my hands, opened it at random, read the middle or the end (I didn't dare show her my contempt at such behaviour) and sat down with a dubious pout. I would go and get another book, and barely had the text held me in its embrace than I heard her nattering on once again about Marie-Rose or Jean-Michel. It was unbearable.

'Don't you like that novel?' I asked her.

'I think I've read it before.'

'What do you mean, you think? If you've eaten a strawberry fool, you know if you've eaten it, don't you?'

'You're the fool!'

And she burst out laughing, delighted at her joke. My look of dismay seemed like a victory. She thought she'd 'nailed me'. I was actually thunderstruck to discover that she could be so stupid.

As she wanted to have her cake and eat it, she bragged about her reading to my parents. They fell for it every time and went into ecstasies:

'You find time to read, in spite of your studies and your bar work?'

43

'You couldn't say the same of Blanche, who doesn't do a thing apart from reading.'

'Do us a favour, Christa: take her books away from her, teach her to live!'

'If it'll be doing you a favour, I promise to try.'

How good she always was at reminding us of our debts to her! Had she secretly lobotomized my parents to make them so stupid? I looked at them uncomprehendingly: did they know that they were constantly denying me? Why did they despise their own child? Had their affection for me been so insubstantial?

But I hadn't given them any problems. In sixteen years, no one had ever complained about me, and I had never criticized them for giving me life, even though it had been short of excitements so far.

I suddenly remembered the parable of the prodigal son: there, in the mouth of Christ, the parents preferred the badly behaved child. *A fortiori*, in the mouth of Christa. Perhaps Christ and Christa were preaching for their own clique: they were the prodigal children. And I was the deplorable *good child*, the one who hadn't been skilled enough to signal, by losing her temper, by running away, being rude, insulting people, how richly she deserved the love of her mother and her father.

The schemer kept her word. She took me to one of those university parties that happen almost every night, organized by one faculty or another, in appalling venues that seem to have been designed as warehouses for old tyres.

It was November, and I was shivering in my jeans. There was a terrible noise going on, a soundtrack dishing out one punishment after another. You had the choice between asphyxiating yourself with cigarette smoke and staying near the open door and catching pneumonia. The foul lighting made the people look even uglier than they were already.

'This is rubbish,' said Christa.

'I agree. Shall we go?'

'No.'

'You just said it was rubbish.'

'I promised your parents I'd take you out.'

I was about to protest when she saw some friends of hers. They came over to see her with their usual gruff effusions. They all started drinking and dancing together.

I felt as though I was in an abattoir but, since my feet were frozen, I pretended to dance as well. Christa had forgotten I existed. I preferred it that way.

All around me, many of the students were drunk. I wished I was, too, but I was too alone to drink. I did my best to move about on the spot. Exhausting hours passed like that, a ludicrous struggle with no end in view.

All of a sudden our punishment changed, administered not with a whip, as before, but with a floorcloth: the slow dance. Boys pounced on girls. An average-looking boy came over and put his arms around me. I asked him his name:

'Renaud. What about you?'

'Blanche.'

Apparently that was enough of an introduction, because

a moment later I found his mouth pressed against mine. Such behaviour struck me as strange, but as I had never been kissed before, I decided to analyze it.

It was bizarre. There was a tongue undulating like the Loch Ness monster against my palate. The guy's arms were exploring my back. It was surprising to feel oneself being inspected, as though one were some kind of monument.

His tourism went on for ages. I began to like it.

A hand grabbed my shoulder and pulled me from his embrace.

'It's late, we're going,' she said.

Renaud gave me a nod of farewell, which I returned.

As we left the place, I noticed that here and there, on the pavement outside, boys and girls were caressing one another in a significant way. If Christa hadn't come to get me, perhaps the same thing would have happened to me – I had absolutely no idea.

No doubt about it, something had happened. I was filled with genuine delight. I was that ridiculous and ecstatic figure: a sixteen-year-old girl who has had her first kiss. Such grandiose follies were worth it.

I didn't say a word. Christa, who hadn't missed a thing, looked at me out of the corner of her eye, apparently thinking that my excitement was as grotesque as things got. No doubt she was right, but I hoped she wouldn't say anything: every creature on earth has a right to its silly little happiness. I was finally experiencing mine; such joys were frail, and it took but a word to destroy them.

Sadly, Christa didn't keep silent.

'Those student parties are like charity shops! Even cast-offs find buyers!'

And she exploded with laughter.

Stunned, I looked at her. She stared right into my eyes and I saw that she was enjoying my humiliation. She laughed all the more.

A thought flashed through my head: *Her name isn't Christa! It's Antichrista!*

That night, as Antichrista was sleeping in what had once been my bed, I tried to bring a little order to the various commotions jostling within me. I went through this mental hubbub:

— It isn't enough for her to steal the little that I had, she has to spoil everything for me! She can see very clearly where to stick the knife, she abuses it, she enjoys giving pain and she has chosen me as her victim. I bring her nothing but good, and she brings me only evil. This isn't going to turn out well. Antichrista, listen to me, you are evil, and I'm going to strike you down like a dragon!

The next moment I heard:

— Stop this delirium, how touchy you are! She just laughed at you a little bit, it doesn't matter, if you were more familiar with friendship you'd know that her ways are perfectly normal, and anyway don't forget that she was the one who took you to that party, without her you'd never have had the courage to go there, and you're happy about what happened to you, it's true that she's a pest, but she's teaching you to live, and whether you want to or not, you needed that.

47

The reply was not long in coming:

— *That's it, you're playing the enemy's game, you always find excuses for her, how much dust are you going to have to bite before you react? If you can't respect yourself, don't be surprised if she doesn't respect you!*

The negotiation went on for ever.

— *So, are you going to demand an apology? You'll look great then, won't you! It would be a better idea not to show her she's hurt you. Rise above it! Don't let yourself get bogged down in your persecution complex!*

— *Coward! Are there any words you wouldn't use as masks for your cowardice?*

— *You're not being realistic. Christa isn't the devil. She has her good sides and her bad sides. She's fetched up in your world, and you wouldn't find it easy to get rid of her. There's one thing you can't deny: that she's life — she's good at living, and you aren't. You should always go in the same direction as life, you shouldn't put up any resistance to it. If you suffer, it's because you're rejecting it. Lower your sights. When you really accept it, your suffering will stop.*

Unable to resolve that internal debate, I forced myself to think about something else. I thought about the stranger's kiss: wasn't it incredible that I'd been kissed? So that boy hadn't noticed that I was a freak! That meant it was possible not to notice: great news!

I tried to remember Renaud's face. Not a single one of his features came to mind. There couldn't have been anything less romantic than that twopenny flirtation, but I didn't care: I asked for nothing more.

48

The next day, Christa told my parents:

'And last night at the party, Blanche had her first snog!'

They looked at me in disbelief. Furious, I said nothing.

'Is that true, Christa?' asked my mother.

'I saw it!'

'And what was the boy like?' my father enquired.

'He was average,' I said soberly.

'He was the first one who came along,' observed Christa.

'That's marvellous,' said my mother, apparently considering this an excellent pedigree.

'Yes, for Blanche, it's not bad,' my father agreed.

All three of them burst out laughing. How happy they were.

For a moment I saw the headline: 'Sixteen-year-old girl massacres parents and best friend. Refuses to explain her actions.'

'So, Blanche, did you like it?' asked my mother.

'None of your business,' I replied.

'Missy has her little secrets,' commented Christa.

Collapse of stout trio.

'Anyway, you have Christa to thank for what happened,' said my father.

The newspaper story formed more clearly in my mind: 'Sixteen-year-old girl massacres best friend, cooks her in a stew, serves to her parents, who are poisoned to death.'

Alone with Antichrista, I surprised myself by talking to her frostily:

'I'd like to ask you not to tell my folks things that don't concern them.'

'Well, goodness me, miss madam . . .'

'You heard me. And if you're not happy about it, you've only to go elsewhere.'

'Calm down now, Blanche! It's okay, I won't say another word.'

And, stunned, she fell silent.

It felt like a staggering victory. Why hadn't I talked to her like that before? Doubtless because I'd been afraid of flying off the handle. And yet I had just proved to myself that I was capable of winning her respect without losing my temper. I would remember that feat, and I hoped to repeat it.

That heroic episode gave me strength for a few days. At lectures or in the flat, I proudly ignored the intruder. When I looked at her furtively, it was to ask myself this question: 'Is Christa beautiful, or is she ugly?'

Insignificant as it might have seemed, it was an extraordinarily difficult question, and one that left me flummoxed. In most cases you don't have to think for a long time to work out whether someone is pretty or ugly: you just know, without having to explain it, and it provides no clue as to a person's mystery. Appearance is only ever another puzzle, and not an especially thorny one.

Christa was a special case. While she certainly had a magnificent body, you couldn't say the same about her face. At first sight, she seemed so sparkling that the merest shadow of a doubt was immediately dispelled: she was the most beautiful woman in the universe, because her eyes glowed with a thousand fires, because her smile was dazzling, because she emitted a crazy light, because the whole of humanity was in love with her. When someone attains that level of seductiveness, no one can imagine that they aren't beautiful.

Except me, right now. Alone of my kind, I knew a secret that Christa, unawares, revealed to me each day: the face of Antichrista – the face of someone who, far from trying to please, saw me as less than nothing. And I noticed that, when she was alone with me, she was unrecognizable: her face, devoid of expression, ceased to conceal the smallness of her washed-out eyes, her pinched lips; her dull physiognomy ceased to conceal the heaviness of her features, the gracelessness of her neck, the inelegance of the oval of her face, the low forehead that demonstrated the limits both of her prettiness and of her mind.

With me, in fact, she acted like a long-married woman who, when her husband is present, no longer worries about walking around frowning, in rollers and a horrible old dressing-gown, keeping for others her charming curls, her flattering dresses and cat-like flirtations. And I reflected bitterly that the long-married man could at least console himself with memories of the time when the delicious creature had striven to attract him; I had had two fleeting smiles, and that was that – why would anyone put themselves out for a clod like me?

When anyone else came into the room, the metamorphosis lasted less than a second; it was spectacular.

Immediately her eyes flashed, the corners of her mouth curled, her glowing features lit up, and Antichrista's mug vanished to reveal – exquisite, fresh, available, idyllic – the girl, the archetype of the barely blossoming virgin, both smart and fragile, the ideal invented by civilization as consolation for the whole of human ugliness.

The equation went like this: Christa was as beautiful as Antichrista was hideous. There was nothing exaggerated about the adjective: hideous was that mask of contempt that was reserved for me and hideous its meaning – you are nothing, you don't deserve me, consider yourself lucky to have me use you as a social stooge and a doormat.

There must have been a switch in her soul that allowed her to turn from Christa to Antichrista. It had no middle setting. And I wondered if there was in fact a common denominator between 'on' and 'off'.

The weekend meant liberation. I lived in expectation of the weekly grail: Friday evening, when the schemer went back to Malmédy.

I lay down on the bed, which became mine again. I rediscovered the greatest luxury on the planet: a room to yourself. A place where you enjoy a royal peace. Flaubert needed a *'gueuloir'*, a 'growlery'; I couldn't live without a *'rêvoir'*, a 'dreamery' where there was nothing and no one, no obstacle to the eternal peregrination of the spirit, where the only decor was the window – when a bedroom has a window, you have your portion of the sky. Why would you want anything else?

I had arranged my bed – the one that Christa had commandeered – so that I could see the sky. I lay there for hours, head on one side, contemplating my share of clouds and blue. The intruder who had taken possession of my bed never looked out of the window: she had purloined my most precious possession.

It was ungrateful of me to deny that Christa had taught me the value of the very thing she had deprived me of: my chosen solitude, my silence, the right to read for whole afternoons without hearing anyone going on about Marie-Rose and Jean-Michel, the intoxication of hearing the absence of sound or, more particularly, the absence of German rock.

I was happy to acknowledge my debt in that respect. But now that my apprenticeship was at an end, couldn't Christa go? I promised not to forget the lesson.

From Friday evening until Sunday evening I left my room only for necessary forays to the bathroom or the kitchen. I didn't spend much time in the latter, pilfering food that could be easily eaten in bed. I saw my parents, the traitors, as little as possible.

I heard them worrying: 'That little girl doesn't come alive when her friend isn't there!'

In fact, I lived *only* when she wasn't there. I had only to sense her presence, and not even next to me – I had only to sense it within a hundred-metre radius, and it didn't matter whether or not she was visible: the knowledge that she was there encased me in concrete until I could barely breathe. In vain I reasoned with myself, saying: 'She's in the bathroom, she'll be there for ages: you're free, it's as if she wasn't there,' but Christa's impact was stronger than logic.

'What's your favourite word?' she asked me one day.

Christa's questions were false questions. She asked me them with the sole purpose of having me ask them back: interrogation was one of the privileged means of her perpetual self-promotion.

Aware that she wouldn't listen to my reply, but docile nonetheless, I replied: 'Bowshot. What about you?'

'Equity,' she replied, detaching the syllables like someone who's just discovered something. 'You see, our choices are revealing: you like a word just for the love of that word; for me, coming from a disadvantaged background as I do, the word must be an idea, one that signifies commitment.'

'Of course,' I observed, reflecting that if absurdity could kill, the intruder would have long since passed on.

At least I agreed with her on one point: our choices were significant. Hers brimmed over with fine feelings: it didn't express any love of language as such, just a girl's desperate need to sell herself.

I was well enough acquainted with Christa to know that she had no idea of the meaning of the word 'bowshot': she would have died, however, rather than ask me. But it was the simplest of words. A bowshot is the distance travelled by an arrow fired from a bow. There wasn't a word in the language with as much power to unleash my dreams: it contained the bow stretched to breaking-point, the arrow and, particularly, the sublime moment of release, the trajectory through the air, the tension towards the infinite, and the chivalric defeat, because despite the bow's desire, its range must be finite, measurable, an *élan vital* inevitably interrupted. The bowshot is the epitome of momentum, from birth to death, pure energy consumed in an instant.

I also came up with the measurement 'a Christa', referring to the extent of the zone that Christa's presence was capable of poisoning. One Christa equalled several bowshots. And there was a concept even larger than the Christa: that was the Antichrista, a cursed circle in which I lived five days a week, with an exponential circumference, because Antichrista was gaining ground before my very eyes, taking over my bedroom, my bed, my parents, my soul.

On Sunday evening, the yoke was donned once more: my father and mother effusively welcomed 'our much-missed girl' and I was expropriated once again.

When the time came to go to bed, there were two possibilities; either Christa looked at me wearily and said in exasperated tones, 'Listen, I don't have to tell you everything,' when I hadn't even asked her to; or, and this was worse, she told me everything, when I hadn't asked her to do that, either.

In the second case I was privy to interminable tales about the bar in Malmédy where she worked, about her most trivial conversations with Jean-Michel, Gunther and the other customers that I couldn't have given a damn about.

She only became interesting when she talked about the subject that secretly excited me: Detlev. I had built up a mythology around this boy, imagining him looking like

David Bowie at the age of eighteen. How handsome he must be! Detlev must be the ideal man: the only one I could ever fall in love with.

I had asked Christa to show me a photograph of him.

'I haven't got one. Photographs are crap,' she had replied.

I found this quite strange, coming from a girl who had papered the walls of my bedroom with posters of her idols. She probably wanted to keep Detlev for herself.

Verbally she was less selective, but it seemed to me that she spoke ill of him, apparently failing to grasp that he was a sacred subject. She talked only about what time they had got up and what they had eaten; she didn't deserve Detlev.

By now, Christa often took me to her student parties. They were always much the same, and the same miracle happened every time: an ordinary, average guy would take a fancy to me.

It never went beyond kissing. When things seemed to be about to degenerate, Christa would tell me it was time to go, and I never argued. I had to admit that her tyrannical attitude suited me: in point of fact, I had no way of knowing whether or not I actually wanted to go any further. My head was just as confused as my body.

But where snogging was concerned, I was still all for it. It was an activity that fascinated me. I was lost in wonder at a form of contact which meant that you didn't have to talk to each other, but which still gave you a unique form of acquaintance with the other person.

They were all bad at kissing, and yet they all kissed in different ways. As for me, I had no idea that they were rotten kissers; I thought it was normal to emerge from a kiss with your nose as wet as though you'd been out in the rain, or with your mouth sucked dry.

In a mental notebook, I jotted down litanies of first names: Renaud – Alain – Marc – Pierre – Thierry – Didier – Miguel . . . That was the edifying list of boys who hadn't noticed that I suffered from a thousand off-putting handicaps. I'm sure that none of them has the slightest memory of me. But if they had any idea what they represented! Each one of them, with his banal and insignificant behaviour, had made me think, in the space of a kiss, that I was *possible*.

It wasn't that they were gallant, affectionate, attentive or even polite. I couldn't help asking one of them (which one? they were so interchangeable) the question that obsessed me:

'Why are you kissing me?'

He replied with a shrug.

'Because you're no uglier than anyone else.'

I can think of a number of girls who would have slapped his face. I, on the other hand, thought it was a fantastic compliment: 'no uglier than anyone else' – it was better than I could have dared hope for in my wildest dreams.

'You've really got the most rubbish love life in the world,' Christa told me after one party.

'Yes,' I replied obediently.

I thought the opposite: from the bottom of my crazed

complexes, I thought what was happening to me was utterly incredible. Cinderella's heart as she left the ball at midnight could not have been as brimming as mine: I was full to bursting.

However much I tried to hide my joy, Christa sensed it and so set about trying to destroy it.

'Basically you're easy. I've never seen you turn a guy down,' she said.

'And it's not as if we get up to much,' I observed, quite rightly.

'How can you settle for so little?'

I couldn't tell her that it all struck me as entirely fabulous. So I said, 'Perhaps because I'm not actually all that easy.'

'Yes, you are. You're easy. You don't know how to play hard to get.'

'Oh, really?'

'You'd never get anybody.'

She flung it straight in my face, and I couldn't quite believe it.

'One day you'll have to bite the bullet. Sixteen years old and still a virgin! The shame of it!'

Christa's attitude towards me was contradictory at the very least. She was still the one who would pull me from the boy's arms just as things were heating up, and yet she never missed an opportunity to stigmatize my scandalous virginity. I couldn't defend myself because I didn't know what I wanted. Without Christa, would I have gone further or not? I hadn't a clue.

It wasn't that I was short of desires: I felt some that were as big as the sky. But what did I desire? No idea. I tried to imagine the motions of physical love with those boys: was that what I wanted? How could I know? I was a blind girl in the land of colours. Maybe I was only curious about acts I knew nothing about.

'You can't compare your case to mine,' I added. 'You've got Detlev.'

'You've got to get your act together and find yourself a proper boyfriend, instead of messing around with anyone and everyone.'

A serious boyfriend: that was a good one. Why not Prince Charming while I was about it? And what was her problem with just anyone? I was perfectly happy with just anyone. I was just anyone myself.

'Are you listening to a word I say, Blanche?'

'Yes. Thanks for your advice, Christa.'

She didn't seem to find my thanks misplaced. The only attitude I could muster towards the intruder was one of absolute submission. Fortunately, deep inside, I wasn't crushed. And Antichrista's sarcastic remarks did nothing to diminish my intoxication at having been kissed by 'just anyone': my pitiful joys were an impregnable fortress.

At least she no longer told my parents of my escapades: that was my sole triumph.

Sometimes I reproached myself for not loving Christa: if I existed at all at university it was thanks to her. Most of the students still didn't know my first name and called me

'Christa's friend' or 'that mate of Christa's'. It was better than nothing. Since I had something resembling an identity, sometimes they would deign to speak to me:

'You haven't seen Christa?' they would ask.

I was Antichrista's satellite.

I started dreaming of adultery: in class, I tried to find someone as lost as I was.

A girl called Sabine seemed to fit the bill. I recognized myself in her: she radiated such unease that she was always alone, because no one wanted to share her discomfort. She gazed at everyone else with the imploring eyes of a starving cat; no one saw her. I immediately told myself off for never having spoken to her.

In actual fact, creatures like Sabine and myself were the guilty ones: rather than approaching their kin and comforting one another, they loved beyond their means – they needed individuals a thousand miles from their own complexes, they needed Christas, radiant and seductive personalities. And then they were astonished that their friendships turned out badly, as though anything like that could possibly work, a panther with a mouse, a shark with a sardine.

I decided to love according to my own low capacity. The mouse went over to speak to the sardine.

'Hi, Sabine. You wouldn't happen to have the notes from the last lecture? I missed a couple of things.'

A look of terror on small fry's face, eyes wide. I thought she'd misheard me and repeated my question. She shook her head frantically, no. I tried again.

'But you were there. I saw you.'

Sabine seemed to be on the brink of tears. I'd seen her? It was more than she could bear.

I realized I'd been clumsy. I tried a different approach:

'Wilmots isn't half boring, don't you think?'

I didn't mean a word of it: he was one of the best teachers we had. It was just a way of being likeable.

Sabine painfully closed her eyes and put a hand on her heart: she appeared to be having some kind of cardiac arrest. I started wondering whether it wasn't out of charity, after all, that no one ever spoke to her.

I was stupid enough to go to her aid.

'Is something wrong? Have you got a problem?'

The sardine, fins palpitating with terror, summoned all her feeble strength and groaned:

'What do you want from me? Leave me alone.'

The whine of a twelve-year-old. Her indignant eyes warned me that if I continued my attack she wouldn't hesitate to resort to drastic measures – she would start disturbing the water, she would quiver her caudal fin; there were no limits to the potential extent of her reprisals.

I walked away, perplexed. Basically, if one saw little friendship among small animals, there was a good reason for it. I had been mistaken in seeing Sabine as my double: she begged, certainly, but she didn't beg people to come, she begged them not to. The slightest contact was torture to her.

'Funny idea, studying political science when you're like that. She'd be better off in a convent,' I thought. At that

61

moment, I saw Christa looking at me with great amusement. She hadn't missed a moment of my attempted adultery. Her eyes told me not to imagine that I could manage without her.

There were mid-year exams in December. The new watchword was: 'Stop laughing. Get to work!' But if I had been laughing, I couldn't say that I'd noticed.

There was no level of pretension that Christa denied herself. We had a general philosophy class that was Mme Verdurin's salon as far as she was concerned: she would adopt an earnest pose to tell us how much more personally Kant spoke to her than he did to us.

'Philosophy is my homeland,' she shamelessly announced.

I took her at her word. After all, German was her first language: that was surely an ideal prerequisite for finding oneself on a level with the universe of Schopenhauer and Hegel. She probably read Nietzsche in the original – admittedly I'd never seen her do it, but that didn't mean anything. When she used the German term to refer to some existential idea, it made me shiver: it sounded more profound that way.

The wonderful thing about exam time was that Christa stopped playing music in the bedroom: we revised in silence. We each occupied half the desk. I watched her studying as she sat opposite me. I had to admire her air of extreme concentration; in comparison, I felt like a scatterbrain.

The time came for the written philosophy paper. The exam lasted four hours, at the end of which Christa exclaimed:

'That was exciting.'

The other exams were orals, in which Christa got much better marks than me. Nothing surprising about that: she was more polished than I was, and she spoke well.

In the oral, the professor gave out the mark as the student left his office. The marks for the written philosophy paper, on the other hand, didn't come out until two weeks later. As soon as they were posted up, Christa sent me off to get them. She also asked me to copy out the marks of all the other students, which was rather annoying since there were eighty of us. I didn't dare protest.

On the way I fumed: 'She has to be certain she's the best! It's pathetic!'

Reaching the boards where the marks were pinned up, I looked for my marks first. Hast: 18 out of 20. I opened my eyes wide: that was more than I'd hoped for. Then I looked for Christa's name. Bildung: 14 out of 20. I burst out laughing. Her face was going to be a sight. I carried out my mission and copied out the list of all eighty students. In doing so I discovered that 18 out of 20 was the best mark and that I was the only one to have got it.

It was too good to be true. There must have been some mistake. Yes, no doubt about it. I tore along to the secretary's office; they told me that Professor Willems was in his office. I ran all the way there.

The philosophy professor irritably welcomed me in.

'I expect you want to query a mark,' he grumbled at the sight of me.

'That's right.'

'And you're Mademoiselle what?'

'Hast.'

Willems consulted his lists.

'You've got notions about yourself. Isn't 18 out of 20 enough for you?'

'On the contrary. I think you've made a mistake in my favour.'

'And you've come to disturb me for that? You must be half-witted.'

'It's just that . . . I think you've switched two results. Couldn't you have got my marks muddled up with Mademoiselle Bildung's?'

'I see. An obsessive seeker after justice,' he said with a sigh.

He picked up a huge bundle of copies and looked up first Hast, then Bildung.

'No, there's no mistake,' he said. 'I give a mark of 14 out of 20 when I'm given back the lecture word for word, and 18 out of 20 for an original opinion. Get out of my sight this minute or I *will* switch the marks.'

I fled in delight.

My joy was short-lived. How was I going to tell Christa? In context, the news was of absolutely no importance: we had passed, and that was what counted. But I guessed that Christa wasn't going to be too pleased. This was philosophy, which was her 'homeland'.

When she saw me, she asked me as if butter wouldn't melt in her mouth:

'So?'

I didn't dare reply, and held out the piece of paper on which I had copied out the eighty marks. She tore it from my hands. She read, and her expression changed. I was surprised by the feeling that came over me: I was ashamed. Having expected to enjoy her disappointment, I felt real pain about it. I was preparing to console her, when she explained:

'It just goes to show that these marking systems are utterly worthless. Everyone knows that I'm the best at philosophy and that you lack profundity.'

This was just incredible. How dare she?

I had a perverse idea, which I immediately began to put into effect. I humbly suggested:

'There must be a mistake. Willems must have switched our results.'

'You think so?'

'Apparently it happens . . .'

'Go and see Willems and ask him.'

'No. It would be better if you went. You see, it would be ridiculous for me to go along and protest to my own disadvantage. Knowing Willems, that might annoy him.'

'Mm.'

She didn't dare tell me that she was going to go and see him. She affected to be above such contingencies.

I laughed up my sleeve, imagining the humiliation she was about to endure.

Two hours later, blazing with fury, she came up to me and said:

'You've been taking the piss out of me!'

'What are you talking about?'

'Willems told me you'd been to his office!'

'Really? You went to see him?' I asked innocently.

'Why did you play such a vile trick on me?'

'What does it matter? Everyone knows that you're the best at philosophy and that I lack profundity. These marking systems are worthless. I don't understand what you're bothered about.'

'Bitch!'

Out she went, slamming the bedroom door.

I heard my father's voice.

'Is something wrong?'

What was his problem?

'It's nothing,' replied Christa. 'Blanche was just bragging because she got the best mark in philosophy.'

'Oh, how petty!' said my mother.

Really, the things people say.

The mid-year exams were over. The next day, Christa went off to spend Christmas with her family. She didn't leave an address or a phone number.

'I just hope she comes back to us!' sighed my father.

'She'll be back. She's left half her things,' I said.

'She's above all this,' my mother observed. 'She isn't like you. She's had better marks than you in all her subjects, and she hasn't gone bragging about it. And here you are boasting about philosophy!'

That took the biscuit! I didn't try to explain what had really happened. I had come to terms with it: whatever I said, my parents would side with Saint Christa.

I KNEW ANTICHRISTA WOULD COME BACK. Not so much for her things as for us. She hadn't finished plundering us. I didn't know what was left on our skeletons to take, but she did.

Two weeks without her: what luxury! I marvelled at the long period of peace stretching out before me.

My parents whinged like teenagers.

'There's no point in Christmas this year. We're forced to be happy. And we're going to have to visit Ursula!'

I lectured them:

'Oh, come on, Aunt Ursula's funny, she's always coming out with the most awful things!'

'As for you, you're not even like a young person. Young people hate Christmas!'

'That's where you're wrong, Christa absolutely loves it, she's more or less German, and as such, she venerates her *Weihnachten*. And could I remind you that it's also her saint's day?'

'That's true! And we can't even wish her a happy one! And she was so angry when she left! Blanche, if you get better results than she does ever again, just avoid gloating.

She comes from a disadvantaged background, she has social issues . . .'

I mentally blocked my ears to their endless nonsense.

Aunt Ursula was our only family. She lived in an old people's home, where she spent her time tyrannizing the staff and passing adverse comments on everything going on around her. My parents felt obliged to see her once a year.

'You look like death warmed up, you three!' the old woman exclaimed by way of welcome.

'That's because we miss Christa,' I said, keen to hear my aunt's reactions on the subject.

'Who's Christa?'

My father, with tears in his eyes, described the admirable girl who now lived with us.

'Is she your mistress?'

My mother took offence: Christa was sixteen, like me. They treated her like a daughter.

'Does she at least pay you rent?'

My father explained to Aunt Ursula that she was from a poor family and that we put her up for nothing.

'Smart kid! She's found a right bunch of suckers!'

'You see, Aunt Ursula, the girl came from far away, from the eastern cantons . . .'

'What? You mean to say she's a German to boot? Aren't you disgusted to have her in your house?'

Outraged protests. 'Such considerations are no longer on the agenda, Aunt Ursula! Things have changed since you were a girl! And anyway, the eastern cantons are Belgian!'

68

I lapped up every word.

When we finally left the old woman, my parents were out of sorts.

'We won't breathe a word of this visit to Christa, will we?'

No, certainly not. What a shame!

It was Christmas Eve. Not being religious, we didn't hold a celebration. We drank mulled wine, just for the pleasure of it. My father sniffed his glass for a long time before saying:

'I expect she's drinking some of this too, as we speak.'

'You're right,' my mother remarked. 'It's very German.'

I noted that there was no longer any need to explain who 'she' was.

My father and mother held their glasses between their hands, as though cherishing them. Eyes closed, they inhaled the fragrant vapour. I knew that through the smells of cinnamon, clove, zest and Muscat, they smelled Christa – if they had lowered their eyelids, it was to use them as a screen on which they saw the girl in the bosom of her family, singing *Weihnachtslieder* by a piano, watching the snowflakes of her remote province falling outside the window.

It mattered little that these images were thoroughly conventional. I wondered what Christa had done to take possession of my parents' soul to this extent and, incidentally, of mine as well.

However much I might have hated her, she haunted me. I constantly collided with her presence inside me. I was worse than my parents: they at least had been invaded by someone they loved.

If only I could love her! Then I would have the consolation of thinking that this misadventure had befallen me as the result of a noble emotion. Besides, my loathing was not so far removed from love: I wanted to love Christa, and sometimes I felt on the brink of that gulf of grace or perdition, at the bottom of which I would have found a way of loving her. Something held me back, something I had difficulty identifying: a critical turn of mind? Lucidity? Or was it merely a desiccated heart? Or jealousy?

I wouldn't have wanted to be Christa, but I would have liked to be loved as she was. I would, without hesitation, have given the rest of my life to see that weakness and that strength, that abandon, that capitulation, that happy resignation to ludicrous adoration light up for me in anyone's eye, anyone at all.

And so, in her absence, Christmas Eve belonged to Antichrista.

She returned to us in early January. My parents' joy was painful to behold.

'It's Epiphany, the day of the *galette des rois*!' she announced, holding up a parcel from the patisserie, containing the traditional marzipan cake.

Christa's coat was removed, she was complimented on how nice she looked, her cheeks were kissed, her two weeks of absence deplored and her cake laid on the table amidst much pomp, next to the gold cardboard crowns.

70

'What a lovely idea!' cried my mother. 'We never think of eating Twelfth Night Cake.'

The girl cut the little *galette* into four pieces. Each of us circumspectly ate our share.

'I didn't get the *fève*,' said Christa, swallowing her last mouthful. She was referring to the little figurines hidden in each cake.

'Neither did I,' said my father.

'It must be Blanche, then,' announced my mother, who hadn't had it either.

All eyes turned to me, as I chewed my last piece.

'No, I didn't get it,' I said, already feeling in the wrong.

'But it can't be anyone else!' said my father furiously.

'Would I have bought a *galette* without a *fève*?' said Christa in astonishment.

'Of course not,' said my mother angrily. 'Blanche eats too quickly; she must have swallowed the *fève* without noticing.'

'If I eat so quickly, how come I was the last one to finish my share?'

'That doesn't mean a thing, you've got a tiny mouth! But you could have paid attention, couldn't you? It was so kind of Christa, and you've spoiled it!'

'This is extraordinary. If someone swallowed the *fève*, why do you insist that it must have been me? It could have been you or Papa or Christa, couldn't it?'

'Christa's far too delicate to swallow a *fève* without noticing!' growled Mama.

'Whereas, clodhopping as I am, I could happily swallow lead soldiers all day long! If that's how I am, maybe I get it from my parents. Which means that the *fève* could just as easily have been swallowed by you or Papa!'

'Come on, Blanche, stop this ridiculous quarrel!' Christa intervened in a peace-making voice.

'As if I was the one who started it!'

'Christa's right,' said my father. 'Stop it, Blanche, none of this matters in the slightest.'

'In any case, Christa is our queen!' announced my mother. And she took a crown and put it on the girl's head.

'That's a bit much!' I observed. 'If everybody's so sure that I was the one who swallowed the *fève* by mistake, then I deserve the title.'

'Then I'll give you my crown, if you want it so much,' said Christa, gazing at the sky, and, with an irritable sigh, she matched the action to her words.

My mother grabbed Christa's wrist and put the crown back on her head.

'That's out of the question, Christa! You're far too kind! You're the Queen!'

'But Blanche is right, it isn't fair!' said Christa, pretending she wanted to defend me.

'How magnanimous you are,' said my father admiringly. 'Don't get involved in Blanche's game, she's being grotesque.'

'May I remind you that it was Mama who started all this?' I asked.

'That's enough, Blanche, we saw you!' my mother broke in exasperatedly. 'How old are you?'

I saw the headline on the page entitled 'Other News': 'A

72

sixteen-year-old girl massacres her parents and her best friend with a kitchen knife over a curious matter involving a *galette des rois*.'

Christa adopted the sacrificial tone of someone who wanted to ease the atmosphere:

'Because I'm the Queen, I need a king. I choose François!'

And she plonked the other crown on my father's head, to his great delight:

'Oh, thank you, Christa!'

'What a surprise! You really are spoilt for choice!' I screeched.

'You're so negative!' the girl said.

'Don't pay her any attention,' my mother continued. 'You can see that she's green with envy.'

'It's weird,' I observed. 'When you talk about Christa in her presence, you say "Christa". When you talk about me in my presence, you say "she".'

'You've got a problem, you know,' my father said to me, shaking his head.

'Are you sure I'm the one with the problem?' I asked.

'Yes,' replied my mother.

The girl got to her feet and, as Christ-like as you could have wished, came over and hugged me:

'We love you, Blanche,' she said with a smile.

My parents applauded the charming scene. I was very sorry that absurdity couldn't kill.

Because the armistice had officially taken place, the improvised celebration passed without a hitch. Never had

Epiphany so spectacularly failed to live up to its name. My parents and I were the procession of the Three Cretins come to hail the one who claimed to be their redeemer. I was horrified to realize the extent to which values had been inverted. If the role of Christ was played by Antichrista, that made me Balthazar, the black King, because my name was Blanche.

In Christian tradition, if one of the three kings is black, the purpose is to show the extent of the Messiah's indulgence. My case was similar: Antichrista allowed herself to be fêted by Blanche, the second-rater. I should have wept with joy at such sublime condescension; I just wanted to weep with laughter.

Gaspard and Melchior distributing their gifts was a sight to see: the gold of their silly affection, the myrrh of their effusions and the frankincense of their admiration for the girl responsible for this imposture.

According to St John, the coming of the Antichrist will herald the end of the world.

No doubt about it: Apocalypse was just around the corner.

The year continued as badly as it had begun. Antichrista just went on extending her kingdom. She encountered no resistance: at university, at home, people saw her as their sovereign.

I had been thoroughly deposed. In my room, Christa had taken possession of almost the whole of the wardrobe: my things had been relegated to the sock drawer, my last fiefdom.

That didn't satisfy my tormentor's need for territorial expansion: the folding bed, on which I was still permitted to sleep, was constantly covered with a jumble of Antichristian clothes.

My parents were seized by a frenzy of hospitality. They searched through antediluvian address books for friends whom they suddenly felt the urgent need to invite to dinner. Any excuse was good enough to introduce Christa to the crowds. Three evenings a week, the flat that had once been so wonderfully peaceful was filled with noisy individuals who appeared to take root there, listening to my parents as they praised Antichrista's countless virtues.

She, showing her most modest of smiles, played the daughter of the house, asking everyone what they wanted to drink and walking around with the plate of canapés. All eyes were on that exquisite creature.

From time to time some buffoon or other would spot me and ask absent-mindedly who the other teenager was.

'Come now, that's Blanche!' the hosts testily replied.

The guests had no idea who I was, and couldn't have cared less. Perhaps they had, sixteen years previously, received a birth announcement that they had quickly thrown in the bin.

It was as though my parents, by promoting Christa, were promoting themselves. They took great pride in accommodating this youthful, beautiful, seductive, irresistible creature: 'If she agrees to live with us, it means that we aren't just anybody.' If they held a salon, it was because they finally had someone to show off.

I wasn't bitter about it. I knew I wasn't the kind of child you can be proud of. The situation wouldn't have bothered me if, in private, Antichrista hadn't been so arrogant in her triumph. I couldn't get over the fact that a girl could be at once so adept and so unsubtle:

'Have you noticed? Your parents' friends adore me.'

Or:

'The guests think I'm your parents' daughter. They can't even see you.'

I didn't react to her provocations.

The acme seemed to have been reached when she announced to me:

'Why do your parents talk so much during those dinners? I can hardly get a word in. They're using me to make themselves interesting!'

Dumbfounded for a moment, I finally said:

'That's intolerable. You should complain to them.'

'Don't be stupid, Blanche. You know very well that politeness forbids it. If your folks were really refined, they'd understand, don't you think?'

I didn't reply.

How could she make such an outrageous remark? Wasn't she worried that I would repeat it to my father or my mother? Of course not: she knew they wouldn't believe me.

So Christa despised her benefactors. I should have suspected as much but, before that declaration, I hadn't been aware of it. That discovery finally unleashed my hatred.

76

Until then, I had not frankly confessed this loathing to myself. I still had a vestige of shame where she was concerned. I told myself that, apart from me, everyone adored Christa: so it must be my fault if I couldn't love her. It was all down to my jealousy and lack of experience: if I had been more practised in human relationships, I might have been less shocked by the girl's strange manners. I had only to learn tolerance.

Now I no longer had any hesitation: Antichrista was scum.

Despite their shortcomings, I loved my parents. They were decent people. They proved it by loving Christa: they were wrong to love her and their love for her was sullied by a thousand human weaknesses, but they really did love her. He who loves is saved.

There was nothing to save Christa. When all was said and done, whom did she love? I could instantly eliminate myself from the list of possible candidates. I had thought that she loved my parents, and now I knew otherwise. As to the famous Detlev, given the offhand manner with which she managed without him I wasn't quite sure that she was all that madly in love. Then there were all the relationships she had at university, the guys she called her boyfriends: I wasn't even all that convinced about them, since they seemed only to serve her personality cult.

I only knew of one person she loved beyond all doubt: herself. She loved herself with uncommon sincerity. I couldn't get over the declarations of love she was capable of making to herself in the course of the most crazed conversations. Thus, one evening, although botanical questions had not even been mentioned, she asked me:

'Do you like hortensias?'

Caught unawares, I thought about those horticultural bath caps for a second and replied, 'Yes.'

She crowed with triumph:

'I knew it! Only unrefined people like hortensias. Personally, I can't stand them. I only like refined things, for I'm terribly refined myself. It's a problem for me: I'm allergic to anything that isn't refined. Where flowers are concerned, I can only bear orchids and *désespoir-du-peintre* – what am I thinking about, you'll never have heard of *désespoir-du-peintre* . . .'

'Of course I have.'

'Really? I'm surprised. That's the flower I'm most like. If a painter tried to paint my portrait, he would end up in despair, he would have so much trouble capturing my refinement. *Désespoir-du-peintre* is my favourite flower.'

How could I have doubted it, Christa, since you are your own favourite.

You couldn't make it up. That's what you call 'showering bouquets'. And isn't there a flower called 'narcissus'?

During this monologue masquerading as a dialogue, I had had to fight against a profound desire to laugh. Christa was very far from laughter: there was no irony, nothing tongue-in-cheek about all the things she said. She was talking about the subject dearest to her heart: the love, the passion, the wonderment, the ardour – the infinite sublimity inspired in her by Mademoiselle Christa Bildung.

A priori, this business had struck me as comical. When it happened, I still believed that she loved other people. I didn't think narcissism was to be condemned when the self-loving person was able to love others as well. Now I was discovering that love was a purely reflexive phenomenon as far as Antichrista was concerned: an arrow fired from the self at the self. The shortest bowshot in the world. Could one live at such small range?

That was her problem. Mine lay in opening my parents' eyes. Their honour depended on it: if she had no qualms about speaking ill of them in my presence, what liberties would she allow herself when I wasn't there? I couldn't bear the idea of my father and mother showing such affection and devotion to someone who despised them.

Half-term fell in February. Christa went home to 'take advantage of the snow' – the expression struck me as worthy of her: if there was snow, then it had to be taken advantage of.

It was time to act.

THE DAY AFTER ANTICHRISTA LEFT, I told my parents that I was going to revise with some friends and that I would be back in the evening. Early in the morning, at the station, I bought a ticket for Malmédy.

I didn't have Christa's address, but I wanted to find the bar where she worked with Detlev. In a town of ten thousand inhabitants, there could hardly be thirty-six thousand such establishments. I brought along a disposable camera.

As the train advanced towards the eastern cantons, I felt my excitement mounting. This trip was a metaphysical expedition for me. I had never taken such an initiative in my life: setting off for a strange place on my own. I looked at my out-going ticket and noticed that there was no acute accent on the 'e' in Malmédy, contrary to the way in which my parents and I had pronounced it. Christa had always said Malmedy rather than Malmédy: so we had been wrong to think of it as a German pronunciation.

The spelling indicated that Christa was right. Without wanting to indulge in cheap psychoanalysis, it was hard not to hear the phrase '*mal me dit*', or 'evil speaks to me', contained in the toponym.

It's true that my raid was not promising. But it would be equally true to say that it was indispensable. The situation could no longer be borne, and I had to know more about Antichrista.

There was no snow in Brussels, but it awaited me in Malmedy. There was something intoxicating about leaving the station and heading off completely at random.

From being metaphysical, my expedition became pataphysical. I walked into every drinks dispensary, leaned on the bar and asked in a solemn voice:

'Does Detlev work here?'

Each time, the bar staff opened their eyes wide in astonishment, before replying that they had never heard the name.

At first, I was reassured by that: if the name was a rare one, it meant that my search would be easier. After two hours of pub-crawling, I began to worry: perhaps Detlev didn't exist.

What if Christa had invented him?

I remembered the episode in which my mother had phoned directory enquiries for the Bildungs' number: the operator had told her that there was no one listed under that name in the region. From that we had deduced that they were too poor to have a phone.

And what if Christa had invented her family?

No, that couldn't be. To enrol at university you had to show an identity card. Her name was Bildung, there was no way around it. Unless she had forged her papers.

In the little Germanic town, the snow was turning into black mud. I no longer knew what I had come in search of. I was cold, and I felt light years away from home.

Street after street, I dipped into the bars and similar establishments. There was a considerable quantity of them. People must have felt the need constantly to move from one to the other in this little backwater with evil in its name.

I found myself outside a dive whose doors were shut. 'We open at five', it said on the door. I couldn't wait that long. It didn't look very promising, and it was highly unlikely that it was the right place. Nonetheless, I wanted to be quite sure.

I rang the bell. Nothing. I did it again, and a fat, fair-haired boy looking like a teenage pig came to the door.

'Excuse me,' I said, 'I wanted to speak to Detlev.'

'That's me.'

I nearly fell over backwards.

'Are you sure you're Detlev?'

'Of course.'

'Is Christa there?'

'No, she's at home.'

Was it really him? It was killingly funny. I tried not to let on.

'Could you give me her address? I'm a friend of hers. I'd like to pay her a visit.'

Completely unsuspecting, the young pig went to get a piece of paper. As he was jotting down Christa's address, I got the disposable camera out and took a few photographs of this legendary character. It had been worth coming all this way to see the David Bowie of the eastern cantons. If he looked like the singer with the different-coloured eyes, then I looked like Sleeping Beauty.

'Are you taking a picture of me?' he asked, astonished.

'It's a surprise for Christa.'

He held out the piece of paper with a pleasant smile. He seemed to be a nice person. I said goodbye, reflecting that I was sure he loved Christa. As for her, if she lied so much about her lover, it must be because she was ashamed of him: which meant that she didn't love him. Had he had a more favourable physique, he might have helped with Antichrista's social promotion. Since he was ugly and fat, she had thought it a good idea to hide him away and tell fibs about him. It was wretched.

I noticed with profound satisfaction that Christa's street was in the town of Malmedy itself: I needed her to live in this place with its evil connotations.

I wasn't surprised that she had lied when she claimed to live in a village: she wouldn't stop at lying, and she seemed to need to blur her tracks.

I wondered what she could have to conceal. What was the secret about her home? The closer I got to her district, the more my curiosity rose.

I couldn't believe my eyes when I saw the house. If the mailbox had not borne the name of Bildung, I would have assumed there was some kind of mistake: it was a well-appointed residence, a lovely big nineteenth-century building, a fine bourgeois home of the kind you would find in a novel.

If these people weren't in the phone book, it was because they were ex-directory. It was easy to guess that they didn't want to be disturbed by just anybody.

I rang the bell. A woman wearing overalls opened the door to me.

'Are you Christa's mother?'

'No, I'm the cleaner,' she replied, as though startled by my mistake.

'Is Dr Bildung there?' I ventured.

'He isn't a doctor, he's in charge of the Bildung factories. So who are you?'

'A friend of Christa's.'

'Do you want to speak to Mademoiselle Christa?'

'No, no. I'm preparing a little surprise for her.'

If I hadn't looked like a child, I think she would have called the police.

I waited for the cleaner to go back inside before, on the quiet, taking some photographs of the house.

I went back to one of the bars I had been into before and asked to use the phone. I looked in the yellow pages and read: 'Bildung Factories: phosphates, chemical products, agrifoodstuffs.' Affluent polluters, then. I copied down the information.

Why had the operator told my mother there was no Bildung family in the area? Perhaps because, in regions where they are economically famous, some names stop being patronyms and become trademarks, a bit like the Michelins in Clermont-Ferrand.

There was nothing more to keep me in Malmedy, the

85

town of evil. I took the train to Brussels, reflecting that my day hadn't been wasted. The snow was erasing the landscape.

The photographs were developed two days later.

When it came to revealing the truth to my parents, I was ashamed. My role in this affair was despicable; I was playing it not because Christa had lied – not all lies are reprehensible – but because I could see no limits to her need to destroy us.

I asked my parents into what had been my bedroom and I told them. I showed the photographs of the lavish Bildung house.

'Are you a private detective now?' my father asked with contempt.

I knew I would be the one whose motives would be called into question.

'I wouldn't have gone snooping around if she hadn't said bad things about you.'

My mother looked distraught.

'It's a coincidence,' she said. 'It's a different Christa Bildung.'

'With a different Detlev as her boyfriend? That's some coincidence,' I replied.

'She might have a good reason for lying,' my father went on.

'Like what?' I asked, almost admiring his need to justify Christa.

'We'll put the question to her.'

'So that she can lie again?' I asked.

'She won't lie now.'

'Why would she stop?' I insisted.

'Because she'll be confronted by reality.'

'And you think that will keep her from lying? On the contrary, I think she'll lie all the more.'

'Maybe she has social issues,' my father continued. 'Rich people get them too, you can't choose where you're born. If she hides it, it's because it's a problem for her. It's not such a serious lie.'

'That doesn't square with Detlev,' I replied. 'He's the only thing in Christa's favour: a decent, fat bloke who couldn't possibly come from a bourgeois background. If she had described him as he was, I would buy your social issues theory. But no, she had to invent a handsome, noble knight. You can see that Christa isn't trying to give a humble and modest impression of herself.'

And I held out a photograph of the Belgian David Bowie. My father looked at it with a hint of a smile. My mother's reaction was peculiar; she uttered a cry of disgust at the sight of Detlev and exclaimed in an indignant voice:

'Why did she do that to us?'

And I knew that Christa had lost an ally. So, in my mother's eyes, it was much more serious to have a boyfriend with a pig-like face than to have tried to soften our hearts with phoney proletarian origins.

'Her fibs about the boy may be ridiculous, but they're kids' stuff,' said my father. 'And anyway, maybe she didn't lie to us all that much: she probably is financing her own studies, so that she won't owe anything to her dad, the big boss. The proof is that her boyfriend isn't a bourgeois.'

'It doesn't stop her living with her parents,' I protested.

'She's only sixteen. She's probably very attached to her mother and her brothers and sisters.'

'Rather than writing our own novel on the subject, why don't we ring up her father?' I suggested.

My mother saw my father's reluctance.

'If you don't call, I will,' she said.

When my father had been put through to M. Bildung, he turned on the speaker.

'So you're M. Hast, Blanche's father,' said a frosty voice. 'I see.'

We didn't know what he saw. At least he seemed to be aware of our existence, which seemed astonishing to me, given the disinformation practised by his daughter.

'I'm sorry to disturb you at work,' stammered my poor father, who was very intimidated.

They exchanged a couple of banalities. Then the boss of the Bildung factories announced:

'Listen, my dear Sir, I am very happy that Christa is staying with you, in a family. In such times as these, it is more reassuring than to imagine her alone and left to her own devices. However, I think you are rather abusing the situation. The rent that you demand is exorbitant. Anyone other than myself would have refused to pay such a sum for a folding bed in a maid's room. It is only because my daughter insisted. She adores Blanche, you see. I know, you are a teacher and I am a company director. None the less, you shouldn't overstep the mark; since you present me with the opportunity, I must tell you that I refuse to accept the raise that you imposed after Christmas. Goodbye.'

And he put the phone down on him.

My father had turned pale. My mother burst out laughing. I hesitated somewhere between the two.

'Can you imagine the amount of money she must have made thanks to us?' I asked.

'Maybe she needs it for a reason we're unaware of,' said my father.

'Are you still defending her?' I cried, offended.

'After the humiliation you've just suffered because of her?' said my mother.

'We haven't got all the pieces of the puzzle,' he said stubbornly. 'It's not impossible that Christa is donating the money to some charity or other.'

'So you think it's okay to defraud people?'

'I just refuse to judge her too easily. Now we know she had a choice. She could have lived wherever she liked. And yet she chose to live with us. So she really needed us, even though we had nothing special to give her. Couldn't that be a cry for help?'

I wasn't sure that it was. That wasn't to say that my father's question was unfounded: why had she chosen our tiny family circle? Easy money couldn't have been her only reason.

My parents' attitude did make me see them in a good light. They had been spectacularly mocked and, if they were disappointed, they were reacting without bitterness. At no point did I hear them express annoyance over the money.

My mother felt betrayed by Detlev's ugliness: it was strange behaviour, but it wasn't petty. As to my father, he was so big-hearted that he wanted to understand Christa's motivation.

The only thing that disturbed me about my father's indulgence was my awareness that it would not have been bestowed on me in a similar case. My parents always behaved as though we had all the duties and everyone else had all the rights, indeed all the excuses. If Christa had lapsed, there had to be a mystery, an explanation, extenuating circumstances, and so on. If I had been the guilty party, I would have received a sound telling-off.

Now all we could do was await the return of the prodigal child.

We no longer spoke of Christa. Her name was now taboo. We had a kind of tacit agreement not to broach the subject unless she was there to defend herself.

I wondered if Christa had any idea what had happened. It was far from certain. If Detlev and the cleaning woman were good at keeping secrets, they might not have told her about my visit. As to the sordid phone call, Monsieur Bildung might have wanted to be gentle with his daughter and spare her the story.

My father was right: there were still some shadowy areas. The main one lay in knowing our role in the whole affair.

As to myself, I also found myself wondering about the enigma that was Detlev: why would a girl as pretentious and ambitious as Christa have chosen a boy like that? A girl who was spoilt for choice, who had handsome suitors

thronging around her, had settled for a decent, plump
bloke. It was true, it made her likeable, but likeable was
hardly the first word that sprang to mind when you thought
of Christa. I lost myself in conjecture.

The prodigal child arrived on Sunday evening. Straight away
I worked out that she didn't know a thing. I felt profoundly
embarrassed when she showered us with her usual effusions.

My parents didn't kill the fatted calf. They immediately
sat down at the table.

'Christa, we phoned your father. Why did you lie to us?'
asked Papa.

Christa froze. Silence.

'Why did you tell us all those fibs?' he insisted kindly.

'Is it money you're after?' she yelled, her voice filled with
contempt.

'We just want the truth.'

'It seems to me that you know it already. What else do
you want?'

'We want to know why you lied to us,' he repeated.

'For money,' she said aggressively.

'No: you could have got hold of that money in other
ways. So why was it?'

From that moment Christa seemed to opt for the strategy
employed by the Marquise von O. In her case it was pitiful.
She acted offended:

'And I who trusted you! And you − you had to go
snooping meanly around the place . . .'

'Don't try and turn the tables.'

'When you love someone, you trust them to the bitter end!' she proclaimed.

'That's all we are asking of you. That's why we want to know why you lied.'

'You don't understand anything!' she raged. 'Trusting someone to the bitter end means not demanding that they explain themselves.'

'We're delighted that you've read Kleist. But we're not as subtle as you are, and we need a little extra information.'

I couldn't get over my father's level-headedness. I'd never heard him talking like that.

'It's not fair! There are three of you and I'm all on my own!' the poor martyr cried.

'It's just what you've been doing to us every day since you've been here,' I broke in.

'You, too!' she cried, like Caesar talking to Brutus on the Ides of March. 'I thought you were my friend. You owe everything to me!'

What struck me was her apparent sincerity. She had convinced herself that she was telling the truth. There were many possible replies to such appalling remarks; but I preferred to let her dig a hole for herself by saying nothing, first of all because it was an effective tactic, and secondly because watching her keep on digging was a spectacle to be savoured in silence.

'If you can't explain why you lied,' my father said gently, 'it may be that you're a mythomaniac. It's an illness that crops up frequently, pathological lying. Lying for the sake of it . . .'

'What nonsense!' she shrieked.

I was staggered to see what a mess she was making of it. Couldn't she tell what an easy time she was being given? She was tangling herself up in her own aggression, the most stupid of strategies. My father was so fond of her that she could have come up with the most unlikely reasons for her behaviour, and she would have got off scot-free. Instead of which she was fruitlessly burning her boats.

My mother had not said a word since the beginning of the altercation. I knew her well enough to know what was going on in her mind: superimposed over Christa's face she now saw Detlev's mug. As a result, she couldn't stop staring at Christa with dismay.

With one final outburst, Christa yelled in our faces:

'So much the worse for you. You're just idiots, you don't deserve me! Let him who loves me follow me!'

Then she dashed to my room. No one followed her.

Half an hour later she re-emerged with her luggage. We hadn't moved.

'You've lost me!' she announced.

Leaving the flat, she slammed the door behind her.

MY FATHER IMPOSED A STATUS QUO.

'Christa hasn't explained anything,' he said. 'In the presence of doubt, let's abstain from judging her. Since we have no idea of her motivation, let us not speak ill of the girl.'

After that, we never mentioned her again.

Christa still attended university, where I proudly ignored her.

One day, having checked that no one could see us, she came over to me.

'Detlev and the maid told me. You were the one who came snooping.'

I looked at her coldly and didn't say anything else.

'You've raped me!' she went on. 'You've violated my intimacy, do you understand?'

'That phrase, "Do you understand?" again.'

And this girl who had forced me to undress, who had mocked my nakedness, was accusing me of rape?

I said nothing and merely smiled.

'What makes you think you can go spying on everybody?' she went on. 'I'm sure you'd love to grass me up to my friends and family!'

'Those are your ways, Christa, not mine.'

She should have been reassured. She had good reason to be worried that I would tell the truth to her father or her gang. But the discovery that I would not descend to that level gave her no consolation: she was aware of my crushing superiority, and she bit her thumb.

'You can play the little princess all you like,' she replied. 'It doesn't sit well with the way you are or with your pathetic role as a private detective. I don't need to ask how much you wanted to hurt me to go to such measures!'

'Why would I take the trouble to hurt you, Christa, when you're so good at hurting yourself!' I remarked indifferently.

'You and your parents must spend your time gossiping about me, I should imagine. At least it keeps you all busy.'

'Inconceivable as it might appear, we never talk about you.'

I turned my back on her and left, enjoying my strength.

A few days later, my father received a letter from Monsieur Bildung.

The blackmail that you have tried to inflict upon my daughter is unworthy. Christa was right to leave your home. Consider yourself fortunate that I do not report you to the police.

'She's doing everything she can to make us react,' said my father, who had read the letter out to us. 'Never mind, I'll never know what blackmail I'm supposed to be guilty of.'

'Aren't you going to call him and tell him the truth?' my mother protested.

'No. That's exactly the reaction that Christa is hoping for.'

'Why? She stands to lose everything.'

'She clearly wants to lose. I don't want her to.'

'And you don't mind the fact that she's telling such awful stories about you?' she insisted.

'No, because I know I have nothing to be ashamed of.'

At university, I had the feeling that Christa's gang now looked at me with utter contempt. I tried to see it as an effect of my paranoia.

But one morning, her dearest friend came over and spat in my face. I knew then that my persecution was not an illusion. I was sorely tempted to grab him and ask him what I had done to deserve his saliva in my face.

At that moment I caught sight of Christa, who was staring at me slyly. And I knew she expected me to react. So I pretended I hadn't seen her.

The vexations continued. My mother received a letter from Madame Bildung. Amongst other things, her prose contained this particular pearl:

My daughter Christa tells me that you demanded to see her naked. I find it regrettable that you are still allowed to be a member of the teaching profession.

As for me, I had the honour of an insult-filled letter from Detlev, who told me that I would die a virgin, for who would want an old trout like me? Witty, I thought, coming from an Adonis such as himself.

If we didn't talk about Christa, I did still think about her. I considered myself better informed than my father about the affair and privately concluded: 'I know what no one knows: her name is Antichrista. If she chose us as a target it's because, in this mediocre world, we are still as unlike her as it's possible to be. She had come to put us under her power, and she didn't succeed: how could she digest such a failure? She still wants to try and destroy herself, with the sole purpose of dragging us down with her. Hence the absolute necessity of our inertia.'

Non-intervention requires more energy than its opposite. I had no idea what Christa told the students about me, but it must have been very serious to judge by the looks of disgust that now welcomed me wherever I went.

I provoked such indignation that even Sabine came to shout at me:

'And to think you tried to have me, too! How awful!'

And the sardine fled, twitching her fins about, and I watched her go, wondering what she meant by the word 'have'.

Antichrista's skill lay in the mystery of her accusations. Most of the time, my parents and I did not know the nature of the grievances imputed to us: it only made them seem all the more abject.

Those who, at university and elsewhere, passed on the stories of our turpitude no more suspected our innocence than they did our ignorance, and although they weren't aware of it, they were acting out a play of rare perversity: they set out to inspire in us the just shame of behaviour whose seriousness we were unable to assess – theft? rape? murder? necrophilia? – precisely in order to make us call them to account.

We stood our ground. It was hard, especially for me, since university constituted the whole of my social life. I was stunned by my misfortune: in my sixteen years of life, I had had only one friend, and she had turned out to be a meta-physical ordeal. I felt that my troubles weren't yet over.

Was there anything Christa wouldn't stoop to? The question kept me awake at night.

I was sure, none the less, like my father, that it was impor-tant to do nothing. Unless I came up with some startlingly brilliant ruse, nothing could drag me from that position – and I certainly wasn't going to attempt a verbal self-defence. To speak would have been to provoke an attack. Silence made me as impossible to catch as a piece of soap: the ever-increasing whispers slipped off my back.

Sadly, inertia did nothing to discourage Antichrista. Her stubbornness knew no limits. I would have to come up with that brilliant feat. Nothing sprang to mind.

If I could even have understood my enemy! But I could see her intentions without being able to cast any light on them. I still didn't know why she had lied to us so much: she was so seductive that she wouldn't have needed to lie in order to twist me around her little finger. And yet her lies got worse than ever.

Was her self-doubt so complete? Perhaps she thought her only way of making people like her was to tell the most outrageous lies rather than simply being herself: she could have been quite endearing, if she hadn't felt the obligation to be so obnoxious. Respect for the truth was not a chief concern of mine, and I could have found her mythomania charming if it had been inoffensive: for example, telling me that Detlev was splendid was an endearing fib. If she hadn't used it with the sole purpose of crushing me, I wouldn't have had a problem with it. Christa's problem was that she couldn't imagine anything beyond power games.

As far as I was concerned, such issues left me bored beyond words. Perhaps that was why I had never had a friend before: too often, at school and elsewhere, I had seen the noble name of friendship attached to obscure serfdoms, to systematic arrangements of humiliation, permanent coups d'état, revolting acts of submission, even scapegoating.

I had a sublime vision of friendship: if it wasn't Orestes and Pylades, Achilles and Patroclus, Montaigne and La Boétie, because she was she, because I was I, then I wanted none of it. If it made way for the slightest hint of meanness, the slightest rivalry, a shadow of envy, the shadow of a shadow, I kicked it away.

How could I have believed that what I had with Christa could have been 'because she was she, because I was I'?

What awful availability within my soul had let her come upon me as a conquered land? I was ashamed at the ease with which she had deceived me.

And yet I was strangely proud of it. If I had been deceived, it was because, for a moment, I had loved. 'I am one of those who love, not those who hate,' declares Sophocles' Antigone. No one has ever said anything more beautiful.

Christa's campaign of defamation began to slide into ostracism. I sometimes felt like laughing at the thought of the weird customs of the Hast family sect.

I discovered that I was more important than I had believed. From seeing myself as the most insignificant quantity in the political-science faculty, I had become the centre of attention.

'Clear off, bitch,' one of my fellow students yelled at me one day.

The bitch wouldn't budge. The students had to put up with my abject presence. Sometimes I endured it all with good humour and threw ogress glares at the others, which always had the desired effect.

Unfortunately, most of the time this little game led only to despondency.

Unhappiness can have its upside: in my case I got back my room and my right to read. I had never read as much as I did during this time: I devoured books, as much to make up for past deficits as to confront the imminent crisis. People who think that reading is an escape are a long way from the truth: to read is to be placed in the presence of the real in its most concentrated state – which is, strangely, less frightening than dealing with its perpetual dilutions.

What I was going through now was an infusion of ordeals, and that was the most painful thing about it – not to be able to grab evil. You are mistaken when you think you read at random: it was now that I started to read Georges Bernanos, the very author I needed.

In his novel *L'Imposture* I came across this sentence: 'Mediocrity is indifference to good and evil.' My eyes opened wide.

I ran to class: I was late. Panting, I tumbled into the lecture theatre: the professor was absent, and Christa had taken advantage of the fact to take his seat and talk about something.

I climbed towards my row, at the top of the steps. As I sat down I became aware of the silence that had fallen as I entered the room: Christa had stopped talking the moment I came in.

All the students had turned to face me, and I realized the crucial subject Antichrista had been entertaining them with. I knew I could never remain indifferent to such evil.

I didn't need to think. I got to my feet and went back down the staircase I had just climbed. Driven by a certainty that made me want to laugh, I walked calmly towards Christa.

She was smiling, convinced that she had triumphed over my patience. Finally, I was going to do what she hoped I would: rail at her, confront her, even slap her; she was going to have her moment of glory, and she was waiting for me.

I took her face between my hands and pressed my lips to hers. I took advantage of the shortcomings of the Renauds, Alains, Marcs, Pierres, Thierrys, Didiers, Miguels, etc., to improvise, with an innate and sudden skill, a gift of tongues, the most absurd, the most useless, the most disconcerting and beautiful thing that humankind has invented: a cinema kiss.

I encountered no resistance. It is true that I had the advantage of complete surprise at my disposal: the utterly unexpected. In this full-on mouth-to-mouth clinch I was sweetness and light.

When I had demonstrated my state of mind for a long time, I pushed her away and turned to face the dumb-founded, beaming lecture hall. A crushing victory. I asked those surplus degenerates:

'Anyone else?'

My bowshot was vast. A spearman of the first water, I could just have picked up eighty halberds and run them all through. But in my limitless indulgence, I merely looked them up and down disdainfully, sliced off a few con-temptible heads with my gaze and left the hall, leaving behind me a poor, shattered victim who had bitten the dust.

It was the day before the Easter holidays.

Christa returned to the bosom of her family. I imagined her nailed to a cross in Malmedy: a seasonal fantasy. My parents and I received no more scurrilous mail.

Two weeks later, lectures resumed. Christa was never seen in the university again. No one asked after her. It was as though she had never existed.

I was still sixteen, still a virgin, and yet my status had changed to an incredible degree. Anyone who had carved herself such a reputation in the field of snogging was worthy of respect.

Time passed. I failed the June exams: my mind was elsewhere. My parents went travelling, warning me that it would be in my interests to pass in September.

I was left alone in the flat. I had never been alone for such a long time, and I was overjoyed: if there hadn't been boring lectures to assimilate, they would have been the holidays of a lifetime.

IT WAS A STRANGE SUMMER. The heat of Brussels was comically ugly, and I closed the shutters once and for all: I settled in darkness and silence. I became an endive.

Very quickly, I learned to see in the dark as though it was broad daylight. I never lit a lamp; the faint light filtering through the shades was enough for me.

My days had no rhythm apart from the waxing and waning of the faint sunlight. I didn't poke my nose outdoors: I had given myself the absurd challenge of surviving, for two months of banishment, on the groceries in the cupboards. The lack of fresh food added to my wretched appearance.

My studies didn't interest me in the slightest. I decided to pass the exams out of pride and then change direction. I imagined the most diverse fates for myself: undertaker, radiologist, halberd-seller, florist, marble-cutter, archery teacher, heating mechanic, umbrella repairwoman, agony aunt, camerawoman, seller of indulgences.

The phone never rang. Who could have called me apart from my parents? They were hurtling down unnavigable rivers, taking pictures of Scotsmen in kilts, contemplating forty centuries from the top of the pyramids, sitting down with Papuans to eat the last family of cannibals – who knows what kinds of exoticism were spicing up their lives.

On 13 August, I turned seventeen. The phone didn't ring then, either. Nothing surprising about that: summer birthdays are never celebrated.

Since seventeen, as we know, is not a serious age, I wasted the morning hours in a kind of mental no-man's-land, at the end of which I pretended to revise for my political-science course. I actually had no idea of the gulf into which my consciousness was hurtling.

Suddenly, in the middle of the afternoon, I felt the urgent need to see a body. There was only one at my disposal.

Like a ghost, I got up and opened the wardrobe, which had a big mirror on the inside of the door. In it, I saw an endive wearing an enormous white shirt.

Since there was still no body, I undressed and looked.

Disappointment: the miracle had not taken place. There was nothing in the reflection that could have inspired love. I philosophically adjusted to the fact: I had never had the habit of loving myself. And besides, it could still happen. I had time.

And then, in the mirror, a sequence of terrible things happened.

I saw the dead girl seize the living.

I saw my arms rising to the horizontal, in a gesture of crucifixion, then my elbows bending at an acute angle, and my hands coming together palm to palm, praying, like a statue, against their will.

I saw my fingers stretching out as if I were an ancient Greek wrestler. I saw my shoulders tensing like a bow, I saw my thoracic cage distorted with strain and I saw my body cease to belong to me and, beyond shame, perform the gymnastic exercise prescribed by Antichrista.

So her will was done, not mine.